FLIGHT OR FIGHT

ADVANCE PRAISE FOR *FLIGHT OR FIGHT*

I couldn't put *Flight or Fight* down! Jane Ray's passionate
and empathetic character kept me engaged from start
to finish. The one question I was left with was,
when will the sequel be ready!?!
— Jackie Ward, Head of Animal Care,
Wildlife Rescue Association of BC

Ms. Haynes has successfully blended a good storyline with
real issues of wildlife rehabilitation into a very readable novel.
Readers will gain knowledge of this relatively unknown field as
well as its wider community implications. I especially liked the
strong individuality and practicality of the girls in
problem-solving an unfamiliar issue.
— Elizabeth Thunstrom, Vice-President,
Wildlife Rehabilitators' Network of BC,
and rehabilitator for 25 years

Diane Haynes has created a world that is as moving and
heartfelt as it is funny and hip. *Flight or Fight* is as vibrant
and fascinating as the animals that inhabit it.
— Brent Piaskoski, Executive Producer,
"Naturally Sadie" (The Family Channel and Disney)

JANE RAY'S
WILDLIFE RESCUE SERIES

FLIGHT OR FIGHT

DIANE HAYNES

Edited by Ian Whitelaw
Proofread by Sonnet Force
Cover photos by Devin Manky, except Siwash Rock by Gertjan Hofman
Author photo by Devin Manky
Cover and interior design by Five Seventeen
Illustration by Five Seventeen

Printed and bound in Canada.

Library and Archives Canada Cataloguing in Publication
Haynes, Diane
    Flight or fight / Diane Haynes.
    (Animal rescue series)
ISBN 1-55285-658-5
    I. Title. II. Series.
    PS8615.A95F55 2005   jC813'.6   C2005-904280-X

The publisher acknowledges the support of the Canada Council and
the Cultural Services Branch of the Government of British Columbia in
making this publication possible. Whitecap Books also acknowledges
the financial support of the Government of Canada through the Book
Publishing Industry Development Program for our publishing activities.

The inside pages of this book are 100% recycled, processed chlorine-
free paper with 40% post-consumer content. For more information,
visit Markets Initiative's website: www.oldgrowthfree.com.

FOR MOUSE

DISCLAIMER

All of the characters and events in *Flight or Fight* are fictional, and any resemblance to any real persons or events is purely coincidental. The animal-related stories are, however, based on the real-life experiences of the author as a volunteer with the Wildlife Rescue Association of British Columbia. Readers should be aware that extensive training as well as specific government permits are required for the keeping and rehabilitating of wild animals, and that the animal rescue and rehabilitation scenarios described in this book are not to be attempted by members of the public. *Flight or Fight* is in no way intended to act as a "how-to" manual for the capture, washing, or treatment of wild birds or animals. Please see Flory's Files starting on page 276 for information on how you can help injured, orphaned, or pollution-damaged wildlife in your community.

CONTENTS

1

RESCUE

IT WAS SUNDAY MORNING IN A RAINFOREST, and a solitary figure was making her way along a path at the edge of the world. The concrete path was gray, and the water below the edge of the wall to her left was gray, because the sky was gray. Ahead of her, where there should have been mountains topped with snow, there was nothing but gray. And on the far west horizon, where there should have been a distant island, named for this city at the edge of the world, there was also only gray. It was raining, not in drops, exactly, but in webs of dew that seemed to materialize out of the fog itself and drape themselves over everything, moving or still. The figure was running. Not from. Not to. Just running.

Jane checked her watch. Twenty-five minutes. She should be passing Siwash Rock on her left. She could see about twenty feet out into the water, but the massive sixty-foot rock with its crowning cedar was hidden behind a curtain of gray. About ten more minutes and she would pass under the Lion's Gate Bridge. That, at least, she'd be able to see.

She watched her breath blend into the fog, and in her peripheral vision she saw her left fist, lightly clenched, come into view, and then her right. Black woolen mitts. She wished she'd worn something colorful, some little beacon, some sign of life. She wished, actually, that a couple of signs of life named Amy MacGillivray and Flory Morales were running beside her. Her best friends had used the weather as an excuse to skip their long Sunday run and spend the day at the mall. Jane smiled to herself, half-wishing she was there with them. She turned her focus back to the soft padding of her running shoes on the wet, worn pavement, the crash of waves against the stone and concrete seawall, and her breath ... in every three steps, out every three steps.

The rhythms were familiar, calming. Jane had been running since she was twelve, and the feeling of her body in motion under its own power and the sound of her breath measuring out her footfalls always brought her back to herself, made her feel strong, as though she could do anything. Ordinarily, she ran the trails near her home on Elfin Lake in Cedar's Ridge, but when school started this year, she had resolved to run the Vancouver International Holiday Half Marathon in December, and that meant long runs once a week, on unforgiving pavement instead of dirt. So every Sunday morning for the past month, she'd trekked out from the suburbs through Vancouver to Stanley Park, a thousand acres of wilderness that jutted out from the western boundary of the city into the Pacific Ocean. The distance around the park by seawall was almost six and a half miles—a perfect quarter marathon.

Shivering now, the morning's chill hinting of the winter to come, Jane lifted her shoulders and dropped them again, letting her arms hang at her sides for a moment before resuming her stride. As she passed under the Lion's Gate Bridge, hearing the cars flying back and forth over Burrard Inlet from Stanley Park to Vancouver's North Shore, she checked her watch again: thirty-seven minutes. Perfect. If she kept up her pace she'd complete her circuit of the park in an hour and ten.

The bird appeared at first to be playing in the waves. A steady easterly breeze was sweeping foot-high swells from the middle of the Inlet into the seawall, and the small black duck bobbed between them, twenty, then ten, then five feet from the wall. When the bird hit the concrete, Jane stopped running, not quite believing what she'd seen. The next wave rolled over the animal, dragging it down and sucking it back toward the middle of the Inlet. Jane watched, not blinking, not breathing, waiting for it to pull its wings out of the water and fly. It seemed to try and then give up. Again, the waves dragged it forward and smashed it against the wall.

Not prepared to watch it happen a third time, Jane tore off her shoes and socks and eased herself over the wall into the ice-cold water. It reached her waist and seemed to cling to her in shiny beads like … oil. When the next wave carried the duck toward her, she reached both hands over its folded wings and plucked it out of the sea. It didn't fight her—it didn't have the strength. She waded toward a set of concrete steps further along the wall, and clambered back up to the path, careful not to loosen her grip. The bird's feathers were slick with oil, and Jane could now see that the entire surface of the Inlet glistened a sickly yellow. She ran back to her shoes and socks, wishing again that Amy and Flory were with her, and hoping someone would happen along with a cell phone or even just an extra pair of hands, but the wall was deserted. Encircling the bird with her right arm, she held her left sweater sleeve in her teeth and pulled her arm out, then slipped the whole thing over her head and wrapped it around the feebly struggling duck. Immediately, it calmed down. Jane placed it gently on the ground, pulled on her socks and shoes, and made some decisions. It was at least thirty-seven minutes back to where she'd parked near the corner of Georgia and Denman, or maybe ten to Lumberman's Arch and another ten to cut through the middle of the park. Soaked from the waist down and with only a cotton shirt on top, she was already shivering, and this bird needed help *now*.

She hoisted her awkward bundle and turned back an edge of the sweater to make sure he was breathing. For the first time she noticed the brilliant orange of his bill and the distinctive white head patches on an otherwise black body. His eye was a perfect black circle in a ring of white. He was beautiful. Twenty minutes, seventeen if she pushed it. She tucked him like a football and started to run.

2

FIFTEEN MINUTES OF FAME

T HE URBAN WILDLIFE RESCUE CENTER was a
wild animal hospital and rehabilitation center
nestled in the woods on the south shore of Aerie
Lake, less than a mile from Jane's home. Access was
by an old winding road that ran between the lake
and the highway, and in thinking back over the few
times she'd traveled it with her mom, Jane couldn't
remember ever seeing another car on it. Today she
zipped by three, pushing her battered old Mazda to
its limits.

The slightly rusty little 1988 sedan had been a
birthday gift from her dad, and had been presented
to her at the end of February in the form of one of
his handmade cards. He'd cut the cardboard out in
the shape of a car, colored it blue, and drawn a little
smiling face with long brown hair on the driver's
side, one arm extended out the window, waving. On
the back, in his neat block lettering, it said FOR MISS
JANE RAY: ONE TICKET TO RIDE. NON-TRANSFERABLE.

HAPPY 16ᵀᴴ BIRTHDAY! LOVE DAD. XOXO

Her parents had proceeded to argue over the gift for the next six months, and Jane had continued to take the bus, as usual.

"Why didn't you discuss this with me, Joe?"

"It's *my* gift to Jane, Ellen. I didn't see the need to discuss it with you."

"But we don't have the money for a car right now, even a used one!"

"*We* don't have to worry about that, Ellen! I'm buying the car."

"With *what*? Another loan?"

"It's fine, Ellen. Just let me handle it."

"Fine. Great, fine. You handle it, Joe. Just don't come running to me for any help on this one."

The car itself had appeared in the driveway in early September. Her mom never mentioned the argument, but insisted Jane load the trunk with blankets and non-perishable food, a first-aid kit, and an animal kennel. "You never know when you might get into trouble on the road, Jane, or who may need your help," she said. The argument had taken some of the pleasure out of the gift, but Jane found she could leave its echoes behind by jumping in the car and flying away.

Rounding the last curve now, she pulled into a small gravel lot filled to its capacity of twelve.

Grabbing the kennel from the passenger seat, she ran inside.

Competent hands took the kennel from her and swiftly transferred it to a back room, leaving her with a form to fill out. She jostled for space at the counter with others who'd arrived carrying more oiled birds. Reaching the line "Type of Animal," Jane hesitated.

"Surf scoter," said a clear, sure voice.

Jane looked up into wide green eyes and a smile, the calm at the center of this storm of activity. The tag pinned to her scrubs read "Head of Animal Care." Jane had seen the woman before. Although she appeared to be in her mid-twenties, she had the air of someone much older.

"Hi, I'm Evie Jordan. Thank you so much for coming in with the scoter. You've been here before, haven't you?"

"Yes, with my mom. I'm Jane." She paused. "Is he going to be okay?"

"It's impossible to say," said Evie directly. "You did everything right, keeping him warm and covered and getting here as quickly as you could. But he's heavily oiled, and he likely sustained some injuries hitting the seawall the way you describe here on the form. He's resting now, and when his stress level decreases, we'll bathe him and feed him. We'll certainly give him every chance."

Evie turned to leave, and Jane blurted out, "What happened?" She was angry now, realizing that her scoter, as she now thought of him, and evidently many others like him, could die.

When Evie turned back to her, her face had changed. She was angry, too. "Canola oil. The stuff you see in your grocery store. Probably fifty tonnes, some time early this morning. We had a reliable tip that the leak started with a corroded pipeline belonging to SeaKing Shipping, but so far they haven't taken any responsibility. Nobody has. And meanwhile, animals are dying." She took a deep breath. "Look, I've got to get back to bathing birds." She looked hard at Jane, as if gauging something in her: "If you think you can keep out of the way, come and watch."

Jane followed her past the examination room, where several small kennels sat atop heating pads, down a hallway, where two washers and dryers spun noisily, to an open room, the walls of which were lined with covered cages, kennels, and small aviaries—the hospital's regular patients. In the center of the room, two volunteers dressed in full rain gear, rubber boots, rubber gloves, and goggles stood at a long table, on top of which sat three plastic washtubs filled with steaming water. At the first tub, one woman held the body of a black and white duck, gently massaging soap into the feathers on its breast, belly, and sides.

The other woman held its bill and scrubbed its head, chin, and throat with a soapy toothbrush.

"This is the most stressful thing that bird will ever go through in its life—even getting killed by a predator doesn't last as long—but it's the only chance it has for survival." Evie talked to Jane, supervised the bathing process, and dispatched new arrivals all at the same time. Jane stood silent, hands clenched tightly together, taking in every detail.

"The oil coats their feathers, destroying their natural insulation and buoyancy. Diving ducks like this scaup, or your scoter, become waterlogged, unable to either hunt for food or fly."

The bathers floated the scaup to one side of the tub, then held its wing open, massaging soap into four layers of feathers. The bird writhed, struggling to pull its head free.

"Your scoter was probably just back from its nesting grounds in the Arctic. Normally they're able to withstand extremely cold temperatures, but once they're oiled, they die of hypothermia very quickly. Or they drown, like yours would have. Or they starve because they can't dive and have to spend all their energy just trying to keep warm."

After soaping the scaup's other wing, the bathers counted to three together and hoisted their patient from the first tub into the second. One volunteer added a dollop of Dawn liquid detergent to her toothbrush and went to work again. At Jane's questioning look, Evie smiled.

"It really is the best thing for cutting grease," she joked, easing the tension a little. "And the company will often donate it if we ask. These bottles were left over from the last canola spill."

"Last spill?" Jane asked, incredulous. "This happens a lot?"

"The Coast Guard estimates a thousand to twelve hundred spills off the BC coast every year. And those are just the ones that get reported," Evie answered. "Yeah, it happens a lot." Jane thought of the sickly skim of yellow she'd seen floating on the top of the Inlet waters, and tried to imagine what a crude oil spill must look like. Her mind balked, not wanting to imagine the animals caught in that chemical chaos.

The bathers had scrubbed the scaup thoroughly again, and were preparing to move him to the third tub. "How many times will they wash him?" Jane asked.

"Until the water comes clean," answered Evie. "We have to get it all now. He'll be lucky to survive this bath. A second round isn't really an option."

Jane noticed that almost thirty minutes had gone by since the bathing process had begun, and wondered how this small facility could possibly handle the numbers that were coming through the front door. As if reading her thoughts, Evie said, "We'll bathe birds until nightfall, and then we'll do laundry all night." She grinned. "The only comfort is that the Cedar's Ridge SPCA is doing the same thing. We just don't have the space—or the hot water!—to care for more than four or five birds at a time. Beyond that, we get them stabilized, as we're doing with your scoter, and then transport them." Evie sighed. "I'd be worried if I thought the admissions were going to continue at this rate, but unfortunately, with every passing day, people like yourself will be finding more and more dead animals and fewer and fewer live ones. The volunteer teams will do three or four eighteen-hour days, and then there will be no more birds to wash."

Jane ducked as one of the volunteers swung a hose up and into a sink at the end of the wash table. The water in the third tub had come clean; it was time to rinse the scaup. "This is the hardest part, on us and on the bird," Evie warned. "If that scaup is going to die of stress, it'll be now."

One volunteer held the bird's head, and the other held its body, and together they angled it tail downward into the sink. The woman holding the hose opened the nozzle full force and aimed the jet of water at the top of its head, careful to avoid its eyes. Next, she opened each wing in turn to its full reach, and supported it from underneath with one hand while rinsing it from the top. Lastly, she rinsed the tail feathers, combing them with her fingers until the water ran clear. Just when Jane thought they were done, they flipped the scaup on its back, legs in the air, and angled it head downward into the sink. They directed the powerful stream of water to the downy feathers on its breast and belly, revealing a delicate keel and a thin, pale, almost translucent skin. The bird was smaller than its feathers made it out to be, but much stronger than it appeared. Stronger, Jane thought, than she felt herself at that moment.

Evie turned to ask Jane if she wanted to stay and watch the tube feeding process, but seeing Jane's face, smiled, and said, "Enough for one day, eh? We'll save the drying and the tubefeeding lessons for another time." Jane tried to smile. "C'mon, we'll fetch your kennel and I'll walk you out."

Jane stepped through the doorway into the middle of a sunny day. The rain had stopped, the fog had lifted, and years and years, it seemed, had passed. A local TV crew had set up a camera at the head of the path, and a reporter was casting about for someone to talk to about oiled birds. His eyes lighted on long, swinging dark hair, mud-soaked sweats, and a face like a thundercloud. "Excuse me, miss, did you bring an oiled bird to the Center?"

There was a moment between his question and the start of her answer when Jane knew without any doubt that this was it. This would be her fifteen minutes of fame, the film clip and soundbite artist Andy Warhol predicted everyone would be granted in this brave new media-saturated world. Unlike some of her friends, she'd never anticipated it, never planned what she'd wear, how she'd smile, or how she might spin her fifteen minutes into the real thing. Fame hadn't much interested her. But here it was. Thanks to a duck. And she was soaked and cold and dirty and angry. And ready. Jane Ray stared into the camera, unblinking, and started to speak.

3

SEAKING SHIPPING PACIFIC

Wayde coyne, Belinda Lee, and Mason Choi huddled around the television in Wayde's cluttered ninth-floor office, watching the screen and listening to Jane Ray name SeaKing Shipping as the perpetrator of a canola oil spill that had turned Burrard Inlet a sickly yellow and left animals—maybe hundreds of them—dead in its wake.

Wayde muttered unintelligibly; Belinda swore loudly and creatively; Mason never took his eyes from the screen.

It was Monday morning, 6:00 a.m., the day after the spill. The three SeaKing executives had been summoned to the corporate head offices on West Pender Street by CEO Alan Coyne to watch a videotape of the previous night's newscast. Wayde pushed Play and Pause alternately on the remote according to instructions emanating from the phone conferencing console on his desk, and the three listened to the senior Coyne explain precisely what damage each statement in the news segment could do to his company, how said damage could affect their jobs, how he wanted them to counter each of those statements to the media, and how they'd better have their story straight, a media release out, and a press conference scheduled by 8:00 a.m.

Wayde Coyne tried to focus on his uncle's disembodied voice as it poured into the room via the speaker on his desk, but he was distracted by the image of the tall, dark-haired girl on the screen, Belinda's perfume at its early morning strongest, and the maple-walnut cruller and coffee in his hands. He sighed, and took a bite of the cruller. It was fresh, crispy on the outside and soft and doughy on the inside, and his taste buds sent an instant message to his brain: *everything's going to be okay.* He chased the bite with a mouthful of Irish Crème coffee—five creams—and felt his brain light up like a pinball machine. It was the best he'd felt since yesterday morning, when the guys at work on the SeaKing dock had called him at home to tell him about the spill.

He'd never meant to stick around long enough to get caught in a crisis. He had, in fact, no idea how he'd gone from wanting to be a poet to being the forty-four-year-old operations manager of a shipping company. Forty-four! And still single, still living alone with Jelly, his butterball brown tabby, still stuffing his poems into drawers and suitcases and Tupperware containers in his parents' house in North Vancouver. The house was a tinderbox; if ever there was a fire, he and Jelly would burn like a warlock and his familiar in the kindling of his own poetry. Wow — great image. He transferred the coffee to his cruller hand and jotted it down on the back of one of his business cards.

His uncle's voice broke through for a moment, reminding him of where he was, and of exactly how he'd ended up on the second rung of SeaKing's corporate ladder. Thirty years ago, a sailboat had capsized in a sudden storm off Vancouver Island's east coast. Two adults—a man and a woman—had drowned. Another man had dragged an unconscious teenage boy to Protection Island and resuscitated him, saving his life. The man and woman were Wayde's parents; the boy, Wayde himself. And his savior, his father's younger brother, Alan Coyne. He owed his uncle his life, and so here he was, paying off a debt that seemed to grow larger every year instead of smaller.

Wayde sighed again and glanced down at his cruller. It was gone. He sighed a third time and wiped his hand on his pant leg, hoping Belinda wouldn't notice. He'd driven to work in his sleep, eaten his breakfast in a parallel universe, and would get through the workday by turning office politics into poetry on the backs of reports and memoranda. He wondered about people who didn't get that it was all a joke, who took it so seriously. Like that little keener accounting kid, Mason. His uncle had hired him straight out of university, offering him an insanely high starting salary and benefits that included a downtown gym membership and a top-of-the-line Personal Digital Assistant. Wayde still used a Dilbert wall calendar, for god's sake.

And Belinda. Sometimes Wayde didn't know if Belinda got the joke, or if she was in on it. Belinda had beaten down Alan's door (and Wayde's, too, at first, before she'd figured out who was really in charge) until the senior Coyne had made her head of PR and media relations. And Wayde had had to agree with him—her PowerPoint shows and her writing samples and presentation kits were impressive. But Wayde wondered what had really sold his uncle: her portfolio or her Asian-blonde looks. The thought made him uncomfortable, and he tried to shut it out, along with her Oslo #10 hair, her incessant gum cracking, and that perfume she always wore. He was pretty sure she was sleeping with the accounting kid, which also made him anxious, like he needed to do something about it, call them in for corrective interviews or something. But of course he couldn't do that. Some days he was pretty successful at shutting it all out. Today wasn't going to be one of those days.

"Before you dig into your second course, there, Wayde, do you think maybe you could, like, take some notes?" Belinda spoke in a voice that was supposed to sound like a discreet whisper, but was calculated to be just loud enough for Alan Coyne to hear. "Just because I'm the media rep doesn't mean the vultures might not land on you, too." She cracked her gum. "You can't afford to smell."

Vultures? Smell? Good lord, what was she on about now? Did she mean the doughnut? Wayde felt his ears grow hot, and hated himself for blushing. He blushed again when she pulled a pen from out of her blouse and handed it to him, warm and perfumey. Like a magician's wand from a pair of rabbits, he thought, and stifled an embarrassed giggle. She glared at him.

The speaker on his desk emitted a deep sigh. "She's right, Wayde," the senior Coyne said, sounding like a patient father. "We've all got to have this story straight."

"Choi, you there?" he asked, suddenly sounding more business-like.

"Yes, sir!" Mason responded without looking away from Jane's image held in pause on the screen in front of him.

"What did we lose?"

"Estimate fifty tonnes, sir," without glancing at

the spreadsheet in his hands.

"Net loss on the oil alone?"

"Forty-seven thousand, nine hundred and eighty dollars, sir," again from memory. Wayde realized with a shock that the kid had managed to put this spreadsheet together some time between Alan's phone call at 4:00 a.m. and this meeting at 6:00 a.m. He made a mental note to remind the kid later about the importance of not skipping breakfast.

"Our cost to reship to the client?"

"Twenty-three thousand, eight hundred, sir."

"Does that figure include a percent discount for delay, Choi?"

"Oh … no, sir, I hadn't calculated in a discount. That would raise it to twenty-eight thousand and eighty-four, sir," checking his mental calculations on his PDA.

"Replacement costs on the cleanup equipment? And wage overages?"

"Thirty-four hundred and fifty, and twelve hundred and ninety-six respectively, sir."

"So we're at eighty thousand, eight hundred and ten, is that right?" Alan Coyne's voice was neutral, masking anything he might have felt about the impact such a loss would have on his family's business.

"That's correct, sir." Mason matched his boss's neutral tone.

The speaker console sighed again. "Push Play, Wayde."

SeaKing's CEO and three senior executives listened as Jane closed out the news segment with the story of her rescue of the surf scoter, and a plea for donations to the Urban Wildlife Rescue Center. Wayde pushed Stop on the remote, cutting off her last word.

The console crackled. "Choi, get on the horn with our insurance folks. If it looks like we can recoup the bulk of these losses, I'd like to start this morning's press conference by offering a donation to this little wildlife center."

"Yes, sir!" For the first time that morning, Mason smiled.

"Are we covered by insurance if the pipeline was all corroded and rusty? The guys down at the dock said it was one of the ones we were planning to trash at year end." Wayde's words hung in the stale air of the crowded office for several seconds before he realized the conversation had stopped. He snapped his head up from his notepad, where he'd been drawing bunnies with Belinda's magic pen, and grasped the import of what he'd said from the looks on Belinda's and Mason's faces and the console's crackling silence.

"I thought," the senior Coyne said slowly, "you told me the line had been punctured by an anchor, or a rock."

Wayde twisted the magic pen in his hands until it snapped in half, splattering black ink across his beige khakis. "That's what they told me. That's what they thought at first. But when they hauled it up, it wasn't ... that's not ... they found..." Wayde stopped. In his first moment of clarity since yesterday's phone call from the docks, he knew there was nothing more to say.

"We will be required to undergo an official investigation," Alan Coyne said, his voice taut like a wire. "Until then, until there is *evidence* to the contrary, the official SeaKing story is that this spill was an accident. Is that clear?" There was a click and the console went dead. For a full minute, the room was silent. And then Belinda started to swear.

"I'll be damned if I'm going to lose all this! I'll be damned if I'm going back to some rat-infested basement suite in Chinatown just because of some bimbo bunny-hugger!" She flung an accusatory finger at the TV screen. "She's lying! When I'm finished with this press conference, she's going to be sorry she ever opened her mouth. No one will remember a word she said. She's history!"

She spun around to face Wayde, who was mentally composing a poem about a battle between rats and bunnies. The word "bunny" had him tittering again. "Come on ... let's *go*!" She shut the lights off with one hand and grabbed Wayde's arm with the other, dragging him out of the office and leaving Mason sitting alone in the dark.

"Mase, you with us?" she tossed back over her shoulder.

"I'll meet you guys at the dockyard," he answered, not raising his voice or turning away from the television. He listened to Wayde's reluctant clump-clump and Belinda's aggressive click-click fade away down the hallway. Then he picked up the remote control from Wayde's desk, rewound the tape and, alone in the dark, watched the whole thing again, without interruption, from beginning to end.

4

DREAM GIRL

JANE LAY STILL IN THE HALF DARK, her fluttering, half-conscious gaze taking in the frame of
her bedroom window, and beyond it a picture made
of shadows, blue on gray on black, cedars, poplars,
maples, and silver birches, silhouettes she knew
by heart. A group of ten or twelve smaller shadows
passed through the frame in the shape of a 'V,' calling
a goodbye. Canada geese on their way south. *You're
late,* Jane thought. *Don't you know it's October?* She
stretched slowly, the air in the room cool against her
face and hands, and gazed down at Sweet Pea and
Minnie curled together, interlocked crescents, warm
against her legs.

She had dreamed. A young woman, tall, dark-
haired, coffee-skinned, confident—the young woman
Jane wished she was—and a little girl, Jane's own
small self, had grasped her firmly by the hands and
taken her to fly. In a kind of formation, a flock of
three, with the dream girl head and shoulders ahead

of Jane and the child just behind her, they had risen almost straight up, a hundred or a hundred and fifty feet, and then leveled out above the tops of the tallest cedars.

The woods ahead appeared to arc over the horizon line and spill down the other side of the world, and the three seemed to fly for a long time, but the lake, sparkling below and just behind them, never passed out of sight.

The little girl and the young woman conversed freely, but Jane was silent. As usual, she'd thought. After a while, though, she realized even her silence was part of the conversation. She hadn't been left out at all; it was as if the two could hear what was in her heart.

When they turned back toward home, Jane looked down to find the lake encircled by all the people of her life, gazing up at her and waving. How wonderful that they can see me, she thought. They'd never have believed all this if I'd told them. As her feet touched down on the boat dock in front of the Ray house, her companions disappeared and she found herself alone. Alone, but not lonely. She was sure she would see them both again.

Remembering the dream now, Jane felt a thrill of excitement, as though she really had learned to fly. At that thought, the events of the day before came flooding back like a video on fast forward, and in an instant she lived through it all again. The seawall run, the drowning bird, the chill of the water, the oil, the feel of the bird's body heat and its heartbeat through her sweater as she ran, the controlled chaos at the wild animal hospital, the TV crews ...

Jane slapped her hands to her face and groaned. Was she *nuts*? She hadn't strung that many words together in public since her sixth grade school play. What had she *said*? And on national television! Since when did national television cover stuff that happened in Cedar's Ridge anyway?

There was a quiet tap on her door. Her mom.

"Come in ..."

"You okay? I heard a strange noise that didn't sound much like a cat's meow," her mom teased as she ran a hand along Minnie's upturned tummy.

"Fine," Jane replied, not playing along. Obviously whatever magic spell had gotten her talking yesterday had already worn off. The excitement she'd felt a moment ago had disappeared, too, as quickly as the companions of her dream.

She watched the smile leave her mom's face and her shoulders lift and fall in a sigh, and she was sorry. Sorry, but at a loss for the right words to make it better. It was their regular morning routine: mueslix with a side of tension, and she was an idiot if she'd imagined anything might be any different today because of what she'd done yesterday.

"Your dad's already at the restaurant and I've got an early meeting with a client downtown, so you're on your own 'til about five. Do you think you could get dinner started after school?" Ellen Ray was the senior promotions director at a high-end communications agency, and her long days often meant take-out or leftovers. A home-cooked meal was a rare treat.

"Mm-hmm …" Jane answered, her unseeing gaze trained on the cedar tops.

"'Why, certainly, mom, I'd be glad to!'" Ellen Ray strode out of the room, the cats rising, stretching, and jumping off the bed to follow her to the kitchen. She kept up her imaginary conversation with her imaginary daughter—the dream girl, Jane thought wistfully—all the way down the hall. "Thank you, darling. You're such a wonderful help to me! 'Oh mother, don't mention it, it's nothing!'"

Jane lay still, staring out the window until she heard her mom's car disappear up the long drive. The tops of the tallest cedars swayed slightly in an early morning breeze, but Jane didn't see them. She was playing a movie of memories in her mind, all scenes and snippets as though someone had forgotten to string them together in a way that made sense. Or at least, that made sense to *her*.

The grand opening of her dad's Mediterranean

restaurant, Cedars, the air redolent with garlic and laughter and music, her dad smiling and flushed from the heat of the kitchen and the pleasure of serving his guests. Herself at twelve in her first spaghetti-strap dress and wedge-heeled sandals, giggling as he handed her a glass of red wine. Her mom, beaded evening bag clutched to her stomach, her face pale and held in a tight smile that didn't quite cancel out the worry in her eyes.

Feeling suddenly like a family of two, when they'd always been three, her dad gone every morning before she woke up and home every night after she'd gone to sleep.

Writing him notes and leaving them where he'd be sure to find them—in his coffee mug, tucked inside his shoe, pinned under a windshield wiper on his car. Discovering the notes he left for her, wrapped around the handle of her toothbrush, folded into the shape of a bird and hidden in a pocket of her knapsack, wrapped in the arms of her favorite old doll.

Noticing her mom never danced around the living room to her disco records any more.

The day she realized her mom had started saying, "Your dad …" instead of just "dad."

The first spring break they didn't take a vacation together, her mom saying, "Your dad's too busy." The second spring break they didn't take a vacation together, her mom saying, "Your dad's too busy, and besides, we can't afford it right now."

Watching from the basement door as strangers drove their camper van away, her mom standing in the driveway, her back to her, recounting the handful of paper money the young couple had traded her for it.

Overhearing her mom on the phone with one of her friends, her voice strained with worry, talking about interest rates and the possibility of losing their home.

Jane trying awkwardly to comfort them both, shyly offering her twelve- or thirteen- or fourteen-year-old's suggestions for making things better—

"Why don't I get a paper route?"

"I could give up my allowance."

"What if we all worked in dad's restaurant? Then it would be successful for sure!"

—and the confusing ache of having them ignored.

Walking in on her dad smashing open the papier mâché piggy bank she'd made him. Swimming sick in a flood of feelings she couldn't name, but that seemed to mirror exactly the look on her dad's face. Knowing in that instant that her childhood dad, and her childhood self, were gone, and that there was no new dad, no new self to replace them.

Her mom and dad carrying on as though everything was normal, as though this was the way life was supposed to be, the only way it *could* be now.

Looking up at her mom, Ellen's face shadowed with anger and frustration, her own eyes pouring tears, as her mom asked over and over, "What's wrong with you, Jane?" "What on earth do you want, Jane?" "When are you going to stop moping about the house and get on with things like the rest of us, Jane?"

Having a hundred thousand things she needed to say, but no answers to her mother's questions, and so, saying nothing.

The evening she ran away, the remains of another silent dinner with her mom heavy under her heart. Taking nothing, deciding on no destination, stumbling through the woods surrounding the lake, crying and not caring who heard, pushing her limbs until they burned, and panting like an animal with the effort until, having twice run the maze of trails circling Elfin Lake, she realized she was not tired at all, but felt in fact an exhilarating calm, a sense of something, at last, being within her control. Crossing the threshold of her basement door, still open as she'd left it an hour before, knowing that from this point forward, she would run every day.

The film of memories flickered to a stop, and Jane found herself once more staring at the tall, old cedars, distinct now against the lightening sky. She turned her head quickly to check the time just as the clock clicked over to 6:45. Late! She leapt out of bed, grabbed her flashlight from the bookshelf and ran to the window, where she instantly spotted the bright white flash beaming its way through the woods and across the lake from the MacGillivrays' house. Lifting her light to respond, she hoped Amy hadn't been waiting too long for the return signal. She turned to the west and faced up toward the top of the ridge to forward the signal to Flory. Immediately, Flory's answer flashed. Done. Now Flory and Amy would exchange signals and the circle would be complete. They'd been saying good morning this way every day since they'd read *Anne of Green Gables* the summer they were ten. Mirrors in summer, flashlights in winter. If one of the friends missed a signal, the other two knew to call. Something was wrong. The full circle meant all was well.

Jane scooped out the litterbox and fed the cats, then headed to the front deck with her cereal. The woods around the lake smelled like autumn but the rising sun felt like summer. The day was going to be warm. She wondered whether anyone at school would have seen last night's news broadcast, and half hoped no one had. She still couldn't quite believe she'd opened her mouth in front of a TV camera. Well, there was no undoing it now. Back inside, she pulled on a shirt and shorts, and headed to the trails to run.

5

THE STRANGER IN THE STUDY

JAKE HARBINSALE slammed the basketball down against the hardwood floor of the hallway, snatched it out of the air with one strong, deft hand, and slammed it down again. He kept his eyes on the ball and his ears on the voices in his father's study, and traveled the length of the hallway in three long strides.

He hadn't planned on coming home for lunch today, but his history class had let out at 11:30 and he didn't have to be back until 1:00 p.m. He'd figured he might as well get in some extra practice on his jump shot before tomorrow night's game. But when he rounded the corner onto Elfin Avenue, he almost changed his mind. A strange car sat in the circular driveway of the Harbinsales' imposing Tudor-style home, and the curtains in the window of his father's study were drawn. These signs always meant the same thing: *somebody* was getting reamed out.

Jake's dad, Rand Harbinsale, was the general

manager of the Cedar's Ridge Golf & Country Club and a member of the Cedar's Ridge city council. Rand's raised voice was par for the course in the Harbinsale household—it seemed to be the hallmark of his dad's way of doing business—but it always put Jake on his guard.

Hesitating, his hand on the brilliant brass knobs of the double red front doors, Jake had decided to play it safe, sneak in the back, grab his basketball from the mudroom, and tiptoe back out to the driveway. But what he heard when he entered the house made him forget all about his jump shot. Rand's voice was raised, all right, but so was the voice of the stranger in the study, and the man was giving it back to Rand as good as he got.

"Get out of dry goods and into canola, you said. Take the company public, bypass the recession, retire sooner, you said. Well, I'll tell you, Rand, it couldn't get any more *public* than this mess. Between shareholders, my staff, and the media calling, I haven't had sleep in forty-eight hours!" The man sounded furious.

"Al, Al, Al, take it *easy*, buddy ..." Jake heard his dad break in with his "your problems can't possibly be as bad as mine" voice.

"Easy? Easy for *you* to say, Rand! You and Donna Lise are the ones that've got it easy. Hidden away here in your private lakeside mansion, meanwhile I'm out there trying to explain what went wrong and keep a smile on my face while I'm at it. Good god, Rand, what am I going to tell Ann? I was going to retire next year. If they hold us responsible for cleanup, it'll ruin us!" Jake could hear the hardwood floor creak as someone paced the length of the study.

"You haven't quite hit the poorhouse yet, my friend," Rand replied in a condescending tone Jake knew all too well. The man's obvious distress coupled with his father's sarcastic response made him wince for the stranger. "Your West Van *mansion*, to use your word, and your fancy yacht and your retirement party aren't in any danger," Rand continued on, his choice of words taking over where his tone left off. "You don't have to tell Ann a damn thing, frankly."

"Now listen, did you let the dock workers go like I told you?" Rand changed the subject, his voice all business now. "Your shareholders'll be waiting for that announcement."

"Yes, yes, Rand," the man sighed wearily. "They're off the payroll as of today. You'll see it in the noon newscast. One fellow—Jim Ellis—tried to refuse his severance package, but he signed the agreement in the end, just like the rest of them."

"Tried to refuse his ..." Rand spluttered. "Idiot. I'd bet you a cool million he's the one that tipped off the animal rescue groups. How else would the Ray girl have known to name SeaKing for the TV cameras?"

Jake had been holding his breath for close to two minutes in order to catch every word. On hearing "the Ray girl," he almost exploded. He knew a Ray girl. He didn't think she knew him, but he sure knew her. He started to let his breath out in a slow hiss and almost exploded again when he heard his older brother jump into the conversation in the study. What the heck was *Randy* doing here in the middle of a workday? And why wasn't *his* car out front? This was getting weird.

"Dad called me this morning about doing a quick stock analysis on SeaKing since last night's newscast, and again after your press conference this morning." Randy Junior was holding forth in the "executive voice" he'd adopted since starting at the brokerage firm and moving to Vancouver's trendy Yaletown district.

"As I expected, you took a hit when the markets opened this morning, but you'd bounced back almost to Friday's levels by 10:00 a.m. Barring any further financial ramifications or legal situations, I think you're going to come out of this smelling like roses."

"That's my boy," Jake heard his father say—a phrase he seemed to reserve exclusively for his super-achieving firstborn. "Now, gentlemen, it's noon. Let's watch that newscast."

"But Rand, we're not finished. Your son just mentioned legal issues, and with the investigation still to come and my operations manager telling me something about a corroded pipeline, I..."

"Oh, but we *are* finished," Rand said in a sinuous voice that made Jake squirm. "I'm going to forget you ever said anything about a corroded pipeline and if you know what's good for you, you will, too. End of discussion."

The television in his dad's study roared to life at full volume, and Jake realized that the news broadcast he was now hearing was somehow a continuation of the conversation he'd just overheard. On the whole, it hadn't made much sense to him. The stranger ran a shipping company that was obviously in trouble —although what did that have to do with his dad? or his brother?—but the urgency of the discussion compelled him to find out more. He turned his attention to a new voice emanating from the television.

"... our own exhaustive investigations, of course, and it's clear the pipeline was punctured by a sinking rock or piece of debris, or perhaps even the anchor of a passing boat. Once again, SeaKing regrets the results of this incident. We've done everything in our means to assist with the cleanup process, and we look forward to making a sizeable donation to those animal groups involved in the rescue efforts." The woman's voice had a seductive quality, Jake thought, like a TV commercial for some toy you don't need but suddenly really, really want.

A male commentator's voice picked up the story. "That was public relations representative Belinda Lee for SeaKing Shipping, in response to allegations that a leaky pipeline led to a fifty-tonne canola spill in Vancouver's Burrard Inlet yesterday." Whoa. So that's why the stranger was freaking out. "Over a hundred oiled animals have been admitted to animal shelters so far, but as the oil continues to spread, wildlife experts say we can expect to see those numbers rise. SeaKing's claim that the leak was the result of outside interference with their pipeline means no one is currently stepping up to cover the costs of cleanup and animal care, and those costs are already in the thousands of dollars.

"Here now is the clip that first turned national attention to SeaKing Shipping, and to the plight of the animals caught … in the canola."

"Damn it, Al, I thought you said they'd stopped airing the Ray girl clip!" Rand shouted, drowning out the TV.

"Well, they didn't show it this morning," the man named Al responded tersely.

At full volume, Jake suddenly heard a voice he'd only heard in shy, quiet tones before. But there was no mistaking that voice. It was Jane Ray.

He slammed the basketball down to the floor—once, twice, three times. He figured he'd better let them know he was coming, but that was all the warning he was prepared to give. In three steps he was in the doorway of the study, all eyes on him, his own eyes locked on the television screen.

It was Jane Ray all right, the one his friends called plain Jane. She was quiet and shy, not part of his crowd, but with her long, swinging dark hair, flashing blue eyes, and a sudden smile that left him tongue-tied in the school hallways, she'd caught his attention at the start of the year, and he found her anything but plain. And at the moment, he had to admit she was anything but shy or quiet, either.

As the segment wound to a close, the faces of Randalls Senior and Junior and that of their guest were grim; Jake's was split with a wide grin. Any girl with that much passion, who could hold her own in front of a TV camera and scare the crap out of his dad at the same time was his kind of girl. His friends would see. Without a word to the men in the study, Jake strode back down the hall, tossed the basketball into the mudroom, and headed back to school, stomach empty, game forgotten, and only one thing on his mind.

6
FLORY OPENS A FILE

"MIND YOUR OWN BUSINESS!" Jane shrieked, laughing, as Amy MacGillivray pushed her into a kitchen chair while Flory Morales held a cell phone up to her nose, pretending it was a microphone. Sweet Pea and Minnie wandered in from the front room to see what the excitement was about. "No comment!" Jane yelled into the microphone. She scooped Minnie up into her arms and held her out in front of her: "Talk to my agent!"

It was a warm Monday afternoon, and they'd stopped at Amy's laboratory (formerly her parents' gardening shed, now fully wired and affectionately referred to as the Shack) on the way home from school to check on one of her more odiferous experiments before taking the trails around to the Ray house on the far side of the lake. The three spent most afternoons at either the MacGillivray or the Ray house, and Flory had been unofficially adopted by both families while her parents were away in the

Philippines on business. Flory was still complaining about the smell in the lab when Jane cut in to tell her best friends that Jake Harbinsale had asked her out.

"WHAT??" Amy yelled, her football-coach bellow a surprise coming out of her short, curvy frame. "Are you SERIOUS? YOU? Jake Harbinsale, star athlete and heart-throb of Cedar's Ridge Senior Secondary, asked *YOU* out?" The petite girl sounded like she was chewing out a ref on the sidelines.

"Gee, thanks, Ame. And do you think you could try that a little louder just to make sure he heard you from inside the school gym?" Jane punched the voluble little redhead in the shoulder. Amy could always be counted on to speak her mind, but she hadn't quite mastered the fine arts of diplomacy and timing.

"Okay, but did you say yes?" Amy tried again, only marginally less loudly. "You always talk about what a snob he is, how he never smiles at you when you pass him on the running trails!"

"Actually, that's exactly what I said to him when he asked me to go out with him," Jane said, grinning back at her stupefied friends.

Flory gasped and covered her mouth. "You did not! You said that to him?" she squeaked out from behind her hands. "Out *loud*?" A slight Phillippina girl with fine, pretty features and a trendily cut sheath of blue-black hair, Flory had grown up in a family of lawyers and doctors, where there was a right—and a wrong—way to do everything.

"Oh, I see!" Amy jumped in, back at full volume. "So your oratorial exploits of yesterday have gone to your head! I approve!"

They'd reached the head of the south trail and were steps from Jane's basement door. No cars in the carport; her dad was at the restaurant, as always, and her mom was still downtown.

"But does he still want to go out with you, Jane?" Flory was really worried now. "Did you eventually say yes? Tell me you said yes?"

Jane held a solemn face for about two and a half seconds, just long enough to get the reaction she wanted from Amy and Flory, and then screamed, "YES! Are you nuts? Of course I said yes! Yes, yes, YES!" The three of them raced up the stairs and into the kitchen, Amy and Flory firing personal, intimate, insensitive questions at Jane with the aplomb of seasoned reporters. Amy seemed to hang out with a different guy every week, and Flory had been dating Mark Co since she was fourteen, but Jake Harbinsale would be Jane's first real date.

"What are you going to wear?" "Where are you going?" "Is he borrowing his dad's BMW?" "Are you going to borrow my padded bra?" "Will you let him kiss you on the first date?" "Do you think he's really over Leila Collins?" "Are you prepared for life as the girlfriend of a famous basketball player?" … until Jane pushed them away, her stomach sore from laughing.

"Hey, speaking of famous," Amy said, grabbing a cola from the fridge, "any news since your little moment in the spotlight yesterday? How's the duck?" She sat down at the table across from Jane, crossed her legs, downed the whole can in a single gulp, and belched the alphabet up to the letter K. Glancing down at the can like there was something wrong with it, she shook her head. "I'm losing it, I swear! I did up to M last week!"

"You're a blight on your Scottish heritage, Amy Airlie MacGillivray," Flory said in disgust, her hand at her nose.

"Are you kidding? I have uncles who would kill to be able to get past F!" Amy hollered, slamming the can down and gulping in air for another go.

"Uh, about the duck," Jane interrupted, getting up to pour two glasses of lemonade. "It's called a scoter, actually."

"Surf scoter, yes," Flory broke in, reaching into her knapsack for a black file folder. Jane noticed what she was doing, and caught Amy's eye. They grinned at one another over Flory's head. Just twenty-four hours and Flory had already opened a docket.

Flory's files were famous among everyone who

knew her. In her apartment at home, she had four tall black cabinets filled with them, and she added a new one every couple of years. Eldest daughter of one half of Morales & Monroy, Barristers and Solicitors, Flory Morales had known how to find out anything about anything—and any*one*—from the time she could read. She loved research, and didn't try to make it sound cool by calling it "surfing the 'Net." It was research, and it was a sacred occupation as far as she was concerned. She seemed to remember everything she read, and what she didn't remember word for word, she could find in a matter of seconds in her files.

She opened the slim black folder and began to read: "Surf Scoter: *Melanitta perspicillata*. From *Birds of Coastal British Columbia*. 'Male scoters are big, black sea ducks. Powerful, robust and big billed, they are the Sylvester Stallones of the duck world …'"

"Jane rescued Rambo?" Amy snorted. Flory silenced her with a look before continuing.

"'They wrench shellfish off underwater rocks with their sturdy bills before swallowing them whole and grinding them up in their muscular gizzards. One wonders how much of the bluish sand along our coasts, made from pulverized mussel shells, has been processed by the alimentary canals of these ducks…'"

"Are you saying they poo blue?" Amy asked, incredulous, and even Jane couldn't help laughing. Flory ignored them both.

"'Originally called scooters, scoters are named for their habit of scooting across the water before they become airborne.'" Jane's smile faded a little as she thought of her scoter's attempts to get its oil-soaked wings out of the water to fly. "'To the more imaginative bird enthusiast,'" Flory concluded, "'the reverberation of their beating wings is reminiscent of the sound of Arabic women ululating.'"

By this time Amy was on the floor under the kitchen table, tears rolling down a face contorted with glee, waving her arms in an unflattering imitation of a scoter and ululating to the best of her limited abilities, having never heard ululating—or even the word ululating—before. Sweet Pea and Minnie had jumped up onto the back of the couch for safety. Jane was hunched over, laughing again, her head under the kitchen table so she could see Amy's performance. Flory sat with her arms crossed and her eyes raised to the ceiling, trying not to smile. At that moment, Jane's mom stepped into the kitchen.

Amy sat up quickly and smacked her head on the underside of the table. "Oh, hi Mrs. Ray," she said, holding her head and choking back a howl. "I was just looking for my contact lens."

Flory and Jane both snorted, which sent the three of them into fresh gales of laughter. Jane's mom hardly seemed to notice. She'd been walking in on scenes like this one for almost sixteen years.

"Everyone at work was very impressed with your TV appearance, Jane," she remarked, dropping her purse and keys on the counter and sifting through the day's mail. "They asked whether I had put you through our media training program, can you believe that? So of course I told them no, that I had no idea you were so articulate."

Jane blushed, trying to enjoy the rare compliment but feeling instead the sting of her mom's last words, and wondering again how she'd managed to find her voice in front of a television crew and cameras when she couldn't even find words to answer her mom. Amy saved her by reseating herself at the table and announcing, "We were just asking Jane about Sylvester, Mrs. Ray. Isn't that right, Flory? So Jane, how is Sylvester?"

"I haven't called the wildlife center yet. I don't know," Jane answered, frowning. "I'm sure he's fine."

"Sylvester's the bird you rescued, I take it?" Mrs. Ray asked, pulling vegetables out of the fridge. "Why don't you girls take a walk down there and see for yourselves? I'll have dinner ready when you get back."

Jane winced, remembering she was supposed to

have started dinner. "It's okay, mom, I'll just give them a call later. I can chop that stuff for you."

"All right, then. Thanks, Jane," her mom answered, grabbing the mail and heading down the hall to her home office. "See you later, girls."

For a minute, the only sound in the sunny kitchen was that of the knife blade slicing through cucumber and hitting the plastic cutting board beneath. The window above the counter faced Elfin Lake, and across the water and through the trees Jane could make out Amy's rambling white farmhouse with its cheery green shutters. She imagined Amy's mom in the kitchen there, making dinner for the whole MacGillivray clan, and then pictured Mr. and Mrs. MacGillivray and Amy and Mike gathered around the big oak table, laughing and talking over one another and slipping scraps to Buster under the table. A soft presence at her feet brought her out of her thoughts, and she looked down to find Sweet Pea weaving her white and gray self between her legs. She crouched down to scratch the top of the small white head.

"I could call the wildlife center for you, Jane, if you're worried," Flory said suddenly.

"I'm not worried, Flory," Jane said, more sharply than she'd intended. "I'm sure Sylvester's okay. Look, I'll call them right now." She picked up the receiver and started to punch in the number her mom kept taped to the side of the fridge.

There was a sudden fluttering at the slight opening of the sliding door leading out to the front deck, and then the scrabbling of claws on hardwood as Minnie, who'd never spent a minute of her short life outdoors, aligned every hair and muscle with some ancient instinct and knocked a surprised chickadee out of the air with one lethal paw. She seized the hapless bird in her mouth and then looked up at Jane as if to say, "*Now* what do I do?"

Flory wrapped her arms around her head and started to scream; she was terrified of birds. Amy leapt to the kitchen closet, yanked out a heavy broom and headed for Minnie, as if she planned on sweeping both animals out onto the deck and over the edge to duke it out in the woods.

Jane blocked her and reached Minnie first, grabbed the little dark gray tabby firmly with both hands and tucked her under her right arm. Startled, Minnie opened her jaws and dropped the chickadee. It lay perfectly still, but its eyes were open and Jane could see its breast rising and falling slightly in time with a rapid breath. Without hesitation, she reached down and grasped the bird in her left hand, and dropped the cat from her right. The bird remained immobile in her hand, light and soft as a crumpled piece of silk cloth, and Jane hoped it was shock, or self-preservation, and not injury, that kept the wild creature from struggling against being held.

Remembering Evie Jordan's praise of her handling of the scoter at the wildlife center the day before, she pivoted, almost knocking Amy down, and reached for the tea towel that hung from the oven door railing. She draped it gently over the chickadee, and then transferred the tiny bundle to her other hand, wrapping the cloth loosely to cover the bird completely. Briefly, she registered that Flory had stopped screaming, and that both of her friends were staring at her now, slightly open-mouthed. She kept moving.

Grabbing an empty shoebox from the top shelf in the hall closet with her free hand, Jane dropped it to the floor and pivoted again, collecting a second tea towel and a pencil in her sweep of the kitchen counters. On her knees, her bundle still held protectively in the crook of her right arm, she lined the box with the tea towel, popped the lid back on, and punched a scattering of holes in it with the pencil. Removing the lid once more, she gently placed the wrapped chickadee on the soft toweling, and then closed the box. Sitting back on the floor, she took a deep breath and let it out in a long sigh. It had been less than two minutes since the chickadee had flown in through the opening in the sliding door.

"I guess you're going to the wildlife center after

all." Jane's mom stood in the kitchen doorway smiling, holding out a ten-dollar bill. "Take this as a donation, and let them know she's been nesting in that birch tree all summer. I'm sure her babies are long gone, but if she's in okay shape, maybe they could send her back with you to release in the front yard." Ellen moved to the counter to pick up with the dinner preparations where Jane had left off.

"Can't you just take her outside now and see if she can fly?" Amy asked, still wielding the broom.

"Minnie might have broken the skin with her claws or teeth," Jane answered. "We have to make sure there's no chance of infection before we just let her go."

"Do birds come in here often, Mrs. Ray?" Flory asked, trying to sound nonchalant. She was still a little pale.

"No, Flory," Ellen chuckled. "This is a first. But I'm going to make sure it's the last time it happens. Jane's been pestering me for ages to put a couple of cardboard hawk silhouettes up on those sliding doors. They stop birds from flying into the glass doors and windows, and I guess we need to stop them from flying into the house as well!"

Wow, Jane thought, so she *had* been listening.

"Maybe you need a big sign out on the deck, too," Amy offered, finally relinquishing the broom to the closet. "Keep Out: Killer Kitty Inside!"

Jane had her wallet and keys in one hand, and the shoebox in the other. "Okay, guys, this is 'animal rescue,' as in 'emergency,' as in 'no time to lose!'" Amy and Flory looked at one another with raised eyebrows and smiles. Something had come over their shy friend in the past twenty-four hours that reminded them of the good old days. They yelled their goodbyes back to Mrs. Ray as Jane took the stairs down to the basement two at a time. "Hustle, people, let's go!"

7
SYLVESTER

JANE FELT A SENSE OF *DÉJA VU* as she filled out the admission form for the chickadee at the Urban Wildlife Rescue Center. She smiled and blushed as she wrote, listening to Amy and Flory tell Evie Jordan the story of how she had rescued the bird from the jaws of death. Amy had a penchant for exaggeration, and in her rendition of the events Jane had performed near-impossible physical feats and risked her very life for the sake of the feathered creature. She glanced up once to catch a smile playing at the corners of Evie's mouth, and quickly looked down, blushing again.

From the corner of her eye she could see another staff person in the room behind Evie, tall and tanned by a life spent outdoors, thoroughly examining the chickadee. He kept the bird's head covered through-out the process, which Evie had explained reduced the animal's stress level, and with large, gentle hands, he carefully extended each wing and then each leg, checking for injuries. He held the bird up, blowing to separate the thin covering of feathers along its keel and breast, and then blew again up and down its back. Jane guessed he was looking for punctures in the skin.

"Bird out!" The loud, sharp call came from the care room down the hall, and before Jane could register what it meant, a large, brightly feathered bird flew into the reception area, narrowly missing her head. Flory opened her mouth to scream, caught a pointed glance from Evie and changed her mind. The exam room door slid suddenly closed, and Evie closed the hall door almost simultaneously, trapping the bird in the twelve-foot-square reception area.

Nodding at Amy, Evie said calmly, "Grab the doorknob and make sure that outside door stays closed until we have the bird. Jane, when I give the signal, I want you to try to send it in my direction."

Jane held herself still and watched the frenzied creature flailing through the small space, colliding first with one window and then the other, hitting the floor and taking flight again only to come up against door and desk and ceiling and wall. She had never seen anything so desperate to be free.

The undersides of its wings were the color of salmon flesh, and the upper feathers were dappled with black stripes on brown. Its breast was spotted with black and bibbed at the upper end, and Jane caught a flash of white beneath its tail as it flew, and a slash of red at its long, narrow beak as it called a startling "kee-eww!"

Evie planted herself behind the desk, a long-handled net in her hand. As the bird headed toward the outside door one more time, she stepped backward as far as space allowed and said, "Now!"

Jane threw her left hand up into the air above Amy's head and directly in the bird's flight path. Seeming almost to stop in midair, it turned itself in an abrupt about-face and raced directly into Evie's waiting net. She pulled it toward her with a sharp scoop of her wrist and closed off the open end with her free hand. Sliding the hall door open with her foot, she passed the writhing bird, net and all, to a volunteer who was waiting on the other side.

"Holy crap, Jane, you guys are two of a kind!" Amy said, letting out the breath she'd been holding. "You could practically work here!" She looked over at Evie: "What the heck *was* that?"

"Northern flicker. Member of the woodpecker family. And she has a point, Jane—we could use more volunteers, especially right now. You could do it as work experience for school." Evie glanced over to smile at Jane and caught sight of Flory. The normally rosy girl was white faced and starting to hyperventilate. "Maybe you two should get some fresh air for a few minutes," Evie said, looking pointedly at Amy. "Jane, would you like to help with the chickadee?"

Amy and Flory stepped outside as Evie slid open the exam room door to reveal the young staffer hunched over a stainless steel operating table, holding the chickadee securely beneath one hand and adjusting an overhead light with the other. "Dan, this is Jane Ray," Evie said casually. "She's going to be your second pair of hands. Jane, this is Daniel Jackson. He's working here part time while he studies to be a vet." With introductions over, Evie left the room.

Jane had a couple of seconds to take in the room—windows on the two outside walls, shelves and cupboards stocked with medicines, syringes, bandages, ointments, a scale, and a couple of microscopes (Amy would love this place, she thought), a whiteboard covered with information that made about as much sense to her as Egyptian hieroglyphics, a counter laden with covered boxes and buckets, each housing a newly admitted animal or bird, and in the corner behind her, a canister and sealed container connected to one another by a plastic hose. Jane realized with a start that this was a mechanism for euthanasia, that not every animal that came to the little hospital got well again. Before she could follow the thought any further, Daniel called her to the operating table.

"Have you done this before, Jane?" he asked, making it clear that it would be perfectly okay if her answer were no. "The most important thing is to keep her head covered. That'll keep her calm." Jane replaced his hands with her own, holding a small cloth in place over the chickadee's head with her left hand and, with a light but firm pressure, securing the tiny body in place against the soft towel that lined the surface of the table. She felt a hot sweat break out on her forehead and under her arms; she was afraid of hurting the bird, but at the same time didn't want to be responsible for another "bird out!"

She could feel its heart beating, so fast it was more tremor than rhythm, and she held her right hand in such a way as to leave room for the expansion and contraction of the slight frame as the bird breathed. "That's perfect," Daniel nodded reassuringly, as if understanding he had two patients now instead of one. "Now have a look there, just at the back of the head. There's one small laceration, not deep at all, no other signs of injury anywhere on the body." He blew lightly on the feathering at the base of the chickadee's skull and Jane saw where the thin membrane of skin had been broken—Minnie's claw, she thought ruefully—exposing the deep red of the flesh beneath, which moved in time with the heartbeat she could feel in her hand. "As I say, not too bad. Although you might want to consider belling your cat." Daniel worked as he talked, filling a syringe with a clear fluid from a bottle on one of the shelves.

"She's an indoor cat!" Jane exclaimed, momentarily distracted. The bird sensed her inattention and tried to break free of her grasp. Jane brought her focus back to the life in her hands. "This is the first bird that's ever been on the same side of the glass as my cat. I don't know how she even knew what to do."

"Instinct is a powerful thing," Daniel said directly. Jane looked up into eyes the color of cornflowers, and quickly looked back down at the table.

Daniel bent toward the chickadee, blew again to part the feathers and let a small amount of the clear fluid fall onto the puncture wound. "Saline solution," he said. "Cleans the wound." He blotted it with the end of a cotton swab, used iodine to disinfect it, and then reached into the fridge for a well-used ointment tube. Removing the lid, he squeezed until a clear blue drop the size of a sesame seed fell on the wound. "Surgical glue," he explained, adjusting the overhead light. "The wound's not big enough for stitches. This stuff binds like Crazy Glue, and fast." He held the drop of glue to one edge of torn skin and carefully extended it across the wound to the other edge. "Done." He put his hands over Jane's, and slowly she pulled herself away from the table. She was sweaty and her heart was racing in time with the chicka-dee's, but she felt utterly elated.

"I'm going to give her some antibiotics and put her on heat for twenty minutes or so, and then you can take her home if you want."

Jane nodded at Daniel, smiling shyly. "Thanks."

Outside, she found Amy and Flory sitting on a wooden bench beneath a gnarled old apple tree in the habitat garden. Flory had her head between her knees and Amy was patting her softly on the back.

"Between the smell in there and My Friend Flicka, or whatever that crazy bird was, our Flory's a little indisposed," Amy explained, grinning over Flory's head.

"I'm never coming here again!" Flory's voice emanated in muffled bursts from between her knees.

"So? How's the chicklet thing?" Amy asked.

"Chickadee," Jane corrected. "Good! We can take her home and release her in the front yard."

"Aaaaand?" Amy persisted. "How's Sylvester? Did you sign on to be the next Dr. Doolittle?"

"Oh my gosh, I totally forgot!" Jane turned and ran back into the center. Evie was on the phone and Jane waited as she finished her call. She looked tired, and Jane could tell from her end of the conversation that the call had to do with the oil spill.

"Damn." Jane jumped as Evie, normally so calm, slammed the receiver into its cradle. She looked up at Jane and shook her head angrily. "They're saying it was an accident, which means no money for us. Not unless somebody can prove otherwise."

"Who, SeaKing?" Jane asked.

"Yeah. You put them in the hot seat with your interview yesterday, and they're pulling out all the stops to get themselves out of it. They've even made some statement about offering some pittance of a donation, like they're god's gift to animal rehab." She shook her head again. "How can these companies get away with it, over and over again?"

The words were out of Jane's mouth before she had time to think. "I'd like to sign up to volunteer here. Maybe I could help somehow." She was beginning to wonder if there were two of her: the real her, and then this version of her that ran around saving animals and volunteering for things.

Evie slapped a form and a pen across the desk and said, "That's the best news I've heard all day, Jane."

Jane grinned as she filled in her contact information and wrote down skills and experiences she thought might make her suited to volunteering at the Center. She'd listed "quiet" as a skill, but was no longer sure if that was true. She wrote about how she and her mom had saved Sweet Pea and Minnie from an abandoned house near her mom's office, and as she was about to hand it back to Evie, remembered to note yesterday's rescue of the scoter.

"Speaking of good news," she said, filling out her medical history, "how's my scoter? We've named him Sylvester." She filled in another couple of lines before noticing that Evie hadn't answered. She raised her head and found Evie looking directly at her, her expression studied and neutral. The head of animal care shook her head, very slightly, and Jane understood.

"Your scoter didn't live through the night," Evie said quietly. "His injuries were too severe. I'm sorry."

Jane stared down at a spot on her application form until her vision blurred. She didn't blink, and she couldn't seem to breathe.

Just what was it she had thought she could do? What exactly had made her think she could help in any way? What had all that jumping in the ocean and running and driving and washing and everything been for? The damn thing had just died anyway, and on top of it she'd made an absolute fool of herself on national television. Just who the hell did she think she was?

The outside door swung open and Amy stood on the stoop. "What is *taking* you? Let's get going!"

Jane kept her gaze trained on the desk as she slid the application form toward her, folded it slowly in four, and shoved it into her pocket. "Thanks," she mumbled, just for something to say, and then she turned and followed Amy out, letting the door swing shut behind her.

8
RELEASE

A LOUD TAPPING MADE HER LOOK BACK; it was Daniel in the exam room, waving and pointing at his watch, and then holding up his hand. Five more minutes for the chickadee, he was saying. She wanted to get into her car and drive, to bolt and run, to disappear. She sat down on the bench next to Flory and bit the inside of her lip to keep from crying.

"Sylvester?" Amy said from behind her. She sensed this wasn't the time to press for details. Jane nodded silently.

She heard the center door swing open and shut, and turned, expecting to see Daniel with the chickadee. It was Evie. She wore heavy leather gloves, and balanced something large and loud on the back of one hand, supporting it with the other. It was draped with a thick towel, but its bloodcurdling screech could only belong to one creature: a hawk. Flory bent over and put her head back between her knees.

"They don't all make it, Jane," Evie said quietly.

The wind stirred the last green leaves on the apple tree to a soft ruffling, and a thrush flew up from the marshy shore of Aerie Lake and disappeared into the tree's craggy depths. "But there's a reason I put in ten hours a day here, day after day, and why a hundred volunteers keep coming back here every week. Before you decide what you're going to do with that piece of paper in your pocket, I want you to know what that reason is."

She turned and headed toward an open space behind the Care Center, a large patch of grass and weeds and garden surrounded by the aviaries and pens that housed the animals reacclimating to life outdoors. Jane dug the toe of her shoe into the dirt and shrugged at Amy as if to say, "Let's get this over with." But Amy was already tagging behind Evie, pestering her with questions about the almost two-foot-high blanketed bird.

Jane felt a hand on her shoulder, and Flory's slightly accented voice spoke softly in her ear. "Maybe the reason is good, Jane. Come, I'll go with you." She took Jane's hand in hers and together they walked the path to the little clearing.

"He was brought in last week with CNS damage—that's central nervous system—after hitting somebody's storm window," Evie was explaining. Balancing the hawk against her upper arm, she pulled a second pair of thick gloves from her scrubs pocket and handed them to Jane. "We injected him with a steroid to reduce any swelling around his brain, and gave him a small dose of antibiotics to prevent the possibility of infection. He's been eating well for the past several days, and he just aced his live feeding and flying tests in the raptor pen. There's no reason to keep him—there's still time for him to find a roost for the night. He's ready for release."

Slipping on the gloves, Jane felt that sweat break out again as Evie moved to transfer the hawk to her. "I'm going to hold his body and keep him covered," Evie said slowly, "and you're going to take his feet with your left hand." Jane glanced down at the long yellow toes that ended in sharp, hooked talons, and her eyes widened. "Put your middle finger between his legs, just above the hock joints, to keep them separated, and wrap the rest of your fingers around his legs." Jane could feel the predator's strength in the wiry legs, and found she needed quite a bit of her own strength to hold them still.

"Now put the flat of your right hand to his back," Evie continued. "I'm going to take my hands away. Good. You're doing great. Now listen carefully, because we only get one shot at this."

Jane felt droplets of sweat run down her forehead and pool in her eyebrows before sliding down the sides of her face. Her arms felt awkward and the hawk was getting heavy. She wondered briefly whether a volunteer had ever dropped a bird before. She didn't dare look at Amy or Flory; she couldn't take her eyes off the hawk.

She listened carefully to Evie's instructions, and then Evie asked her to repeat them back to her, step by step. Once the rehabilitator was sure Jane understood what to do, she stood back, and motioned for Amy and Flory to do the same. "He's got a wingspan of about four feet. Give him space."

With a deep breath, Jane steadied her hands. In a swift movement she'd visualized perfectly as Evie had described it, she bent her knees, dropped her arms, and swept the towel off the bird like a magician revealing the results of his sleight of hand. Then she threw her left arm into the air with all her strength.

The hawk was in flight before she finished, and her hand sailed empty through empty sky. For just a moment, she felt as if she'd gone with him. She kept her gaze trained on the red and white and brown of him, her mouth open with the effort and the joy of the release. He circled the whole of Aerie Lake, at times beating his enormous wings against the warm afternoon air, and then resting, sailing, floating, swooping, and starting again. He was playing, Jane thought, trying everything out after a week spent in a cage. Flexing his freedom.

He was looping back now, and passed the shoreline to circle directly above the little clearing. He screeched that unmistakable call, almost as if to say something to the four people gathered below, and then turned again and flew hard to the north, until Jane could no longer distinguish him from the trees on the mountains, or the sky.

When she finally came back to earth, Jane turned to find Daniel standing behind her, shoebox and chickadee in hand. "Two in one afternoon—not a bad day's work."

She smiled then, and looked up at Evie. Stripping off the gloves, she reached into her pocket, pulled out her volunteer application, and handed it to the grinning staffer. She traded the gloves for the chickadee box, and the five headed to the front of the Care Center.

"Where are the TV cameras when you need them?" she joked, her heart still pounding.

Amy whooped. "Hoooooooooo, boy! Look out, SeaKing! Baby's back and she's after your ass!"

9

CINDERELLA MAN

A RIVULET OF COLD SWEAT gathered at the small of his back and trickled down between his buttocks, to pool in the seat of his pants. Wayde squirmed. He was crouched behind the dumpster at the entrance to SeaKing Shipping's dockyards and warehouse in North Vancouver, well camouflaged against the dark October night in a black turtleneck, black wool pants, black toque, and black gloves.

It was Monday, less than an hour before midnight, and the breezy warmth of the autumn day had given way to a blue-black stillness that carried sounds across impossible distances. Wayde watched a murder of crows steal across a screen of moonlit clouds like music across a page—playing my song, he thought. It seemed he could hear the flapping of their wings and every high, ragged caw, although they had to be at least half a mile away.

He'd dressed in front of the full-length mirror in his bedroom, with Jelly in audience at the end of the bed. It was their Monday night ritual, except that usually he was costuming himself for his role as the Cleric in a weekly game of Dungeons & Dragons. He'd begged off tonight, claiming his cat was sick. He'd even parked his car in front of the vet's office for half an hour to lock down his alibi. He'd seen enough movies to know how this worked.

At 11:00, he'd turned off all the lights in the house and crept out to his car, hoisting a large, lumpy duffel bag into the back seat. He coasted down the driveway and onto the street, waiting 'til he'd rounded the corner onto Lonsdale Avenue before firing up the engine and flipping on his headlights. A quick detour for fries and a chocolate milkshake and then he was cruising down the hill toward the water, grooving to the theme song from *Mission Impossible* and two-fisting his midnight snack. He steered with his knees, mixing mouthfuls of food with loud whoops and shouts of "I'm da man!" It crossed his mind that the spy lifestyle might just be his ticket out of shipping.

His bravado had melted—along with about ten pounds of body mass, he was sure—by the time he arrived at the terminals. He'd gone to synchronize his watch and it had hit him that there was no one to synchronize *with*. He was in this on his own.

Well, that was how his uncle must feel, he reminded himself. That's why he'd decided to do this in the first place. Time to shoulder a little of the responsibility, let his uncle know he had his support. Maybe, Wayde thought, maybe even pay him back, finally, for saving his life all those years ago.

Alan Coyne had arrived at the SeaKing dockyards that morning in time for the press conference, and then ensconced himself in the offices at the back of the warehouse where, one by one, he'd fired each of the dock workers that had been on shift at the time of the oil spill. Shortly before noon, looking tired and defeated, he'd left Wayde to take care of the paperwork and gone to placate one of their major shareholders who'd been phoning every fifteen minutes all morning long. He'd returned to their downtown offices that afternoon looking ashen and—Wayde realized for the first time—old.

To Wayde, his Uncle Alan was manly charm, handsome athleticism, a perennial suntan, and pastel leisure suits year round. He made everything look easy, including success at business, and he could beat men much younger than himself at tennis and golf without seeming to break a sweat. He lived to sail with his wife, Ann, and treated Wayde like the son he never had, naming him as his successor in the business long before making any mention of retiring. When he walked into the SeaKing offices that afternoon, Wayde had understood: if his uncle lost

SeaKing Shipping, he would lose his uncle.

The plan had come to him the same way his best poems did: complete, flawless, and inspired. Before leaving the office for the day, he'd stopped in to see his uncle, and said, "Everything's going to be okay, Uncle Al. I promise." It had torn at him to see the hope rise in the older man's eyes. For the first time in his life, he'd felt like the grownup in the relationship, instead of a helpless little boy.

That feeling flooded him again now, along with a rush of adrenaline and a bolt of queasiness as the fries and shake settled into a mass in his gut. He glanced back across the railroad tracks, scanned the length of the terminals, and then looked over to the old warehouse, where a single pot light illuminated the entrance in a wan yellow glow. No night security—they'd been fired, too, and Wayde had made sure to start the new night shift Tuesday instead of tonight. It was now or never.

He hefted the duffel bag, breaking into a sweat again, and half dragged it across the concrete to the warehouse entrance. Three keys in three locks and he was inside, the door closed behind him, the warehouse a black cavern that he knew like his own home. He reached down for the duffel bag and suddenly it occurred to him that the alarm hadn't been triggered when he came in. Another shock of adrenaline coursed through him until he realized he hadn't changed the code and hadn't taught the new guys the old one. They must've had to close up this afternoon without setting the alarm. He breathed again.

By feel and by memory, he made his way to the rear of the warehouse, where the offices were, and let himself into the large storage room. The smell hit him before he could find the light switch: salt water, rotting barnacles, seaweed, and kelp, and underneath it all the grainy scent of canola oil. He flicked the switch and lit up a disaster zone.

Lengths of pipeline lay strewn haphazardly on a plastic tarp, hundreds of feet of hose held together by reinforced steel joints. And the rust of the corroded joints was as obvious as bloody wounds on the smooth silvery surface. His breath came in short, shallow gasps as he took in the magnitude of SeaKing's responsibility for the first time. His responsibility. How had he possibly missed this on last inspection? This kind of damage didn't just pop up in a few weeks. He shook his head, reminding himself he'd have to worry about that later, and set to work.

With an efficiency and speed that came with having worked at every job in the company at one time or another, he removed the corroded joints and placed them carefully at one end of the tarp. Next, he replaced them with the newer, intact joints he'd brought with him, and then rejoined these to the pipeline segments. He used a hammer and chisel he'd brought with him to make a small perforation in the metal, in the center of one of the healthy joints. Finally, from the duffel bag he pulled the old anchor he'd taken from the wall of the den in his parents' home, hoisted it above his head, and brought it down in a controlled drop, with perfect aim, crown point to perforation. It tore easily through the metal, leaving a ragged gash that couldn't be mistaken for anything other than what it was—damage caused by a dragging anchor.

Wayde was covered in oil and breathing hard with the exertion. He was grinning, though, and did a little dance among the pipeline segments to celebrate—his plan had worked perfectly.

So far. Now to get the hell out of here. He loaded the rusted joints into the duffel bag along with the anchor, and turned to switch off the lights. His gloves gleamed with oil and he swore, stripping them off and stuffing them into his pants pockets. He hadn't brought a second pair. He panicked until he realized his fingerprints were all over these light switches anyway, all over the warehouse, for that matter. He didn't need gloves any more.

He was half way back to the warehouse door when the crash came. His body went hot and then ice cold, and he stood paralyzed, imagining the possibilities: armed burglar, vagrant, police detective, psychopathic murderer. He didn't know which terrified him most. Before he could decide, the warehouse door swung wide, letting in a shaft of moonlight that silhouetted a tall figure as it leapt through the doorway and ran in the direction of the road. Wayde registered, "male, baseball cap," before the door swung shut and he slumped to his knees in the dark. "Damn squeegee homeless kids," he muttered to himself as he got to his feet. But he wasn't sure. Not with three locks on the door and the alarm shut off. He wasn't sure at all.

The clock tower at the Quay struck midnight just as he started up the car. Cinderella, he thought, and wondered what slip-up the intruder might have made that would provide a clue to his identity. Ah well, he'd leave that little mystery for tomorrow. Mission accomplished. He was back in spy mode now, his success making him giddy. He cranked the stereo and headed home to Jelly, and to bed.

10
JANE WRITES A LETTER

LESS THAN AN HOUR INTO HER TRAINING SESSION at the Urban Wildlife Rescue Center, Jane was convinced she'd made a mistake. Not since working on a science project with a group of grade seven boys had she heard so much talk about feces. It was Saturday morning, a week after the canola spill, and staffer Daniel Jackson was leading a group of six new volunteers on a tour of the site. In addition to Jane, there was a retired couple who'd decided to volunteer together, and three grade twelve students Jane recognized from Cedar's Ridge High. As they walked through the Center, he told them a little about each of the animals in care, about their injuries and treatment plans, their unique diets and caging requirements, and about the potential hazards of coming in contact with certain species in particular, and with wild animal feces in general. There were, it seemed, a hundred and one possible ways in which a wild animal rehabilitator might accidentally sicken, injure, or kill herself, and another hundred ways at least to harm the animal patients in your care. The tetanus shot she'd endured earlier in the week was the least of it.

"If I forget to shake out the towels and blankets before throwing them in the washing machine, I could be sending small birds and mice to a watery death," she told Amy and Flory later. "And if I don't wash my hands often enough, or if I forget and chew my nails, I could end up with diarrhea and vomiting from salmonellosis. Heck, if I just breathe in invisible airborne particles of feces, I could end up with pneumonia from chlamydiosis or a fungal infection called aspergillosis. And how would I know? Until it was too late! I get bitten by the wrong flea, I've got the plague. By a tick, and I've got lyme disease, which can lead to neurological abnormalities."

"More than you've got now, you mean," Amy chimed in.

Jane glared at her. "They have a contest going for how many times each volunteer's been bitten by a gull. I could get sprayed by a skunk, and if I accidentally forget that I'm not supposed to handle bats or mammals, I could be foaming at the mouth with rabies within nine months!"

"Yeah, well, unless those other neurological abnormalities kick in first," Amy offered helpfully, "that's not something you're likely to forget."

"Wait! I'm not finished!" Jane sputtered. "Daniel told us how he was getting ready to anaesthetize a squirrel once, and mistakenly shot anaesthetic right into his eye! He couldn't move that eyeball for over an hour! And how a barn owl hooked its talons into his arm, and he couldn't just yank them out, because the four toes open and close as a unit, and if you pull on one of them, you break the owl's foot. He had to wait with this owl literally attached to him until someone could pry all four toes loose at once."

"Hate it when that happens," Amy nodded.

"Was this all in the same day?" Flory wailed, simultaneously mesmerized and horrified. She was scribbling furiously in one of her black file folders.

"Oh, man, Flory, I don't think so," Jane answered, before going on. "Oh yeah, and Evie told us about some poor rehabilitator she heard about at a conference who decided he didn't need to wear his goggles while he was handling a juvenile great blue heron. You know, those huge, prehistoric-looking birds with an eight-inch bill? Like a dagger?"

"What happened?" Flory whispered, her hands pressed up against her mouth.

"He stared the heron down, moved in to grab it from its kennel, and it stabbed him right through the eye and pierced his brain." Jane looked around, quite pleased that she had her listeners riveted. "Instant death."

"Never try to stare those herons down, eh?" Amy nodded sagely.

Jane sighed. "Thanks to the fact that my shoulder has been aching for two days from that tetanus shot, at least I don't have to worry if I hook myself on a rusty nail."

"Small blessings," Amy agreed.

In the end, though, the animals themselves won out, and Jane knew that in spite of the risks, she *was* hooked.

Daniel led the trainees through the old house that sat adjacent to the Care Center on the UWRC property. Built in the 1920s, it had been someone's home at one time, but now housed the organization's administration offices upstairs, and a staff and volunteer lunchroom downstairs. Behind the two main buildings, on the land stretching north toward the shoreline of Aerie Lake, lay the intricately designed structures that housed the animals who had been inside the Care Center, and who were now reacclimating to life outdoors. They were relearning to hunt and fly, and to regulate their body temperatures in the outdoors, and they were spending as much time as possible away from human contact.

Daniel reminded his trainees several times throughout the morning that the animals they would be working with were wild, and that the only chance they had of making it after being released was if they stayed wild. "It's called habituation," he explained. "Given the chance, animals will learn that *you* are their source of comfort and food. Some—like crows and ravens—habituate extremely quickly. Others—like ducklings and goslings—can actually imprint on you, and will behave as though you are their mother." The two grade twelve girls giggled. Daniel frowned. "And if that happens, those animals will never make it in the wild." The giggling stopped.

"Wild animals are meant to be wild, and if you take that away from them, you've robbed them of the essence of who and what they are." Jane watched Daniel's hands move as he spoke, the color rising in his face and his blue eyes flashing, and saw that he was passionate about this. "It's one of the hardest decisions we ever have to make here," he said, "but if we believe an animal can't survive in the wild, whether because of injury, or imprinting, or irreversible habituation, we will euthanize that animal."

The little group was sober and silent. Daniel softened his tone. "There's nothing wrong with wanting to cuddle animals, or talk to them and comfort them, or give them names. It's an impulse that comes from caring about them, and that's why all of us are here. But with *wild* animals, that instinct in us is actually a mistake. The SPCA always needs more dog walkers and cat care volunteers, and that may be the place for you," he said, looking directly at the two grade twelve girls. "It takes a certain kind of person to care about these ones," he said, sweeping his arm to indicate the Care Center and the outbuildings, and the trees and the lake and the mountains behind him, "and to hold that impulse in check. For their sake."

On the way back to the Care Center, Daniel pointed out the habitat garden and the workshop used by the volunteer maintenance crew, and Jane began to understand that this hospital would not run, these animals would not be protected, if it weren't for volunteers. A hundred, Evie had said. Working in the Care Center, in the garden, on building repairs, in animal transport, and in the office. It would matter that she was here.

Inside, two experienced volunteers were quietly making the rounds. As they moved slowly through the tasks of feeding and cleaning, Jane felt at first that there seemed to be almost nothing going on in the room. Neither the volunteers nor the animals made any noise, and all of the cages were draped with white sheets, so none of the animals was even visible.

But then Daniel reached into a large metal cage, wrapping a pale gray rock pigeon in a soft cloth, and handed it to her to hold. He wrapped and handed a bird to each of the trainees in turn. The small bundle in her hands was warm with life, and Jane could feel the rock pigeon's steady heartbeat against her fingertips. As she sought to find the best grip on the bird, it sensed her uncertainty and struggled, trying to break free. At once, she was reminded of her scoter, that surprising combination of strength and vulnerability, as an animal whose every instinct was wired for freedom submitted to captivity because of an injury. *Do you understand?* she wondered. *Do you know we're trying to help?*

The rock pigeon went still in her hands, and she took it for an answer. And suddenly the quiet, bare, starkly lit room came alive in her mind. Everything was happening here below sound levels, behind the cotton drapes, without words. This silence, this hearing things that weren't being said, this sub-sonic communication, this was familiar. This was what it was like for her at home. All the unspoken feelings, the reading between the lines, the strange, quick inner conversations that took place constantly between people who didn't really talk to each other any more. This she understood. In four years of keeping silent, Jane realized, she had learned to listen.

And now she heard the ache and fear and confusion of this bird in her hands that had hit a window and had wound up here, one of the lucky ones. And the varied thrush in the corner, bound in a wing wrap, torn by a house cat. And the heron in the kennel on the floor, hit by a car as it rose suddenly from a marshy ditch by the side of the road, ignoring its food and fighting pain and struggling to stay alive in a strange, small, dark container it could not comprehend. Jane heard them all. The room was alive.

"When your cat or dog is sick or injured," Daniel was saying as he placed Jane's rock pigeon back in its cage, "it'll tell you. It'll whimper, or limp, or cry if something hurts. But not these guys. Their life depends on not letting a predator know anything is wrong. Predators go for the weak ones, the injured ones. So when you're handling an animal, take it easy. They're here because they're hurt, but they're not going to remind you of that fact. You're going to have to remember." Jane knew now that she couldn't possibly forget.

Daniel showed them a floor pen designed especially for oiled water birds with their sensitive webbed feet. Right now, it housed only one—a lesser scaup, one of the last of the oiled animals still being housed indoors. Jane caught Evie's eye as she came into the room, and the senior staffer nodded. "That's the scaup we were washing when Jane was here last weekend," she said to the group. "With some of these birds, we get eighty to ninety percent of the *world's* population coming through this region. It's not just whether this scaup lives or dies—although I'd guess that's pretty important to *him*." Evie's grin was forced. "This oil spill will affect the whole species."

Jane realized suddenly that she'd been taking mental notes as Evie talked, and composing a letter to SeaKing Shipping in her head. Write to SeaKing? Well, why not? She'd told Evie she'd try to help. And that donation the company had promised the day after the spill still hadn't arrived. If people at SeaKing knew what was happening to these animals, Jane was sure they'd drive a check over in an instant.

Daniel led them past Isolation Rooms 1 and 2, the intensive care units of the Care Center, and finally back to reception. "Everybody, this is Anthony Lau, our part-time receptionist and transport volunteer dispatcher extraordinaire," Daniel said, introducing them to a tall, slim man in his mid-thirties with a shock of long, straight black hair that hung over his right eye. "Anthony, this is Jane Ray, Ashleigh Peyton, Siri Singh, and Cam Davis, all from Cedar's Ridge High, and Oliver and Martha Hastings."

"Peace, newcomers! Welcome to the fold." As Anthony offered each of them a handshake, Jane heard a now-familiar cry from one of the volunteers in the Care Room—"Bird out!"—and saw an equally familiar northern flicker making straight for front reception.

Immediately, Anthony launched into a disco rendition of "Freak Out!" changing the words slightly to suit the occasion. "Aaahhhhh … *Bird Out!*" As he sang, he clapped his hands and danced around the tiny reception area, sliding the hallway door closed and then turning two quick spins behind the desk before closing the exam room door. "Le freak, c'est chic, bird out. Yeahhhhh … *Bird Out!*"

"Don't mind him," Daniel laughed. "He's just one of those weirdos who likes his job. Now, I'm going to assign you your regular shifts." He went through the list of trainees, ending with Jane. "Jane Ray … I've got you down for … let's see, Thursday mornings, eight 'til noon, with work experience credits for school. Evie's the senior staffer on Thursdays, and hey! You'll be working with Avis!"

Jane couldn't believe her ears. Avis? Was Daniel nuts? How could anyone sound excited about working with Avis? She couldn't think of anything worse.

Avis Morton ran the Care Center kitchen with a grimace and a meat cleaver. Tall and elegant, with perfect posture and impeccable, silver, bobbed hair, Avis dressed for her shift in a tailored shirt and sweater, rolled up at the sleeves, brown tweed pants, and gardening clogs, none of which had a speck of feces on them anywhere. She was, Jane guessed, about a hundred and twenty-five years old. "Avis has been with the UWRC for, what, fifteen years now?" Daniel had said when he introduced her to the trainees. "She was in the Canadian Navy during the war and then taught home economics and cafeteria cooking, so she runs a tight ship," he joked. "She's going to give you your kitchen orientation. Avis, take it away!"

Jane spotted a blood-and-fish-covered carving knife and cutting board on the counter behind Avis and blurted out, "Man, it looks like somebody was murdered in here!"

"That's what happens when you don't rinse your dishes before putting them in the sink," Avis retorted. Jane blushed furiously as the others in the group laughed nervously. "Now gather round, I want to show you how the diet manual works." The group of eight stood shoulder to shoulder in the tiny space as Avis flipped through a thick binder mounted over the counter. In alphabetical order, each page named a different type of bird and listed its individual diet requirements. Some birds ate nothing but seed and grit, others ate protein mix and worms as well as seed, and still others ate fruit as well as larger seeds and even nuts. Menus for the raptors—the birds of prey—included things like mice, rats, and smaller birds, and Jane was just beginning to register what that might mean when Avis yanked open the refrigerator door.

Fruits and vegetables in the crisper drawers, buckets of protein mix and chopped fish on the shelves. Suet, protein drinks, and mashed egg yolk in the door. And in the freezer, cubes of bloodworms, trays of mice, ziplocked bags of rats, and plastic containers of quail. Ashleigh went pale, and Cam dashed out the kitchen's back door to throw up. Avis rolled her eyes. "Life takes life," she said sternly, slamming the fridge door closed. "Animals eat to survive. Only humans have perfected the art of taking more—much more—than we need." She glared directly at Oliver's rather portly midsection.

"If you think of any kitchen-related questions later, don't hesitate to leave a message for me on the lunch-room bulletin board," Avis finished. "I'm always here to help."

Your kind of help I do not need, Jane had thought. And now here she was assigned to Avis's shift! She was about to ask Daniel if he would mind switching her to a different day—she could pretend something had come up at school—when the reception door opened and in walked a small, fair-haired girl bundled in a red duffel coat and pushing a covered doll buggy. Her mother followed her through the door, and the pair reminded Jane of her own mother and herself, and all the times they'd brought birds to the UWRC.

As Anthony gently wheeled the buggy into the exam room, and the group at reception listened to the girl's story, Jane forgot all about changing shifts.

"We went for a walk at the beach today," she said, glancing back at her mom, "and I took my dolls over to hear the waves. That's when I saw those birds." 'Those birds' were five green-winged teals, similar to mallards but much smaller, covered in canola oil. "They were on the sand, just shivering and shivering. I didn't know why. But they looked like they were going to freeze to death! I just knew I had to get them warm again." Her mother had suggested they call someone for help, but the girl had looked around and seen no one nearby who could come to the rescue quickly enough. So she took the clothes off her dolls and wrapped them around the teals, one at a time, carefully covering their heads and then placing them in the buggy, one facing the left side, the next facing right. "It helped them calm down," she said. Daniel just shook his head in amazement.

"Will they be all right?" she asked, gazing up at him from the far side of the counter.

He walked around the desk, crouched down next to her, his eyes level with hers. "You couldn't have done a better job of rescuing those birds," he said. "They're very sick, but we're going to take good care of them. They have a chance because you did the right thing."

She smiled then, and seemed satisfied with Daniel's answer. "May I have my dolls' clothes back, please?"

Out of the corner of her eye, Jane saw Anthony in the exam room holding up a tiny white dress, blue sash hanging limply from the waist. It was almost translucent with oil. Anthony was shaking his head. The little girl's mother, who could see him from where she stood, said, "I think the birds are going to have to keep those clothes to get warm, Sadie. I'll make you some new ones, how about that?"

Sadie looked at Daniel and then turned to gaze up at her mom. "It's okay if the birds need those clothes, mom. My dolls can have blankets for now."

Anthony wheeled her buggy back out to reception, and they all said goodbye to the pair. "Well! I guess that about concludes our training session for today," Daniel said, still shaking his head. "If you folks do half as well as Sadie, you'll make stellar volunteers!"

Jane took off for home at a jog. Amy and Flory, and probably Jake as well, were waiting for her at Cultus Lake, and she still had to pack her bag. But they'd have to wait an extra half hour. She had an email to write to SeaKing Shipping Pacific.

...She was eight years old and she knew how to do the right thing. The staff and volunteers at the UWRC have been "doing the right thing" around the clock for the past week. Resources are running low, and we could really use that donation you offered last week. Thank you for promising to do the right thing, too.

Sincerely yours,
Jane Ray

She hit Send, and then hopped into the little Mazda and headed for Highway 1 east.

11
GOD OF THE SEA

"Oh, sweet mother of mercy, Jane ... it's Jake!"

Jane grabbed the field glasses from Amy's hands and held them up to her eyes. Sure enough, the kayaker they'd been watching for the past ten minutes was Jake Harbinsale. She shook the binoculars like a kaleidoscope and peered through them again, grinning.

He was doing Eskimo rolls, difficult at the best of times and not your natural choice for an October afternoon ... unless you're an athlete. His head broke the surface, short dark curls escaping from beneath his helmet and streaming with water, then his upper body, every rib and ripple of his slim torso defined by the black wet suit and dancing with droplets of sunlight. Spare and strong, he was like an animal, Jane thought, nothing wasted, everything efficient, designed to move in perfect rhythm with nature.

"He's a god!" Flory squealed, taking her turn on the field glasses. Jane and Amy laughed. Jane could see Jake just fine now without any magnification. He was almost at the boat dock. "Jane, you're dating a god! The god of the sea!"

Dating. Jane's stomach suddenly did its own Eskimo roll. That's right. This wasn't just some silly, pining long-distance crush any more. She whacked Flory on the shoulder. "Quick, put the binoculars down, Flory, or go watch that crow. He's going to see us staring at him like we're spies or something!"

On the dock now, Jake secured his kayak and ran his hands through his hair to wring out the lake water. He'd probably be beautiful just brushing his teeth, Jane thought. "He wears that wet suit well, don't you think?" Amy inquired, reaching over to snap the strap of Jane's bathing suit top.

"The thought had crossed my mind," Jane answered with a mischievous smile. "But shouldn't you be paying more attention to Eric Fabbro's wet suit?" Eric was Amy's date *du jour*.

"For one thing, Eric's not here yet," Amy retorted. "And for another, he wouldn't be caught dead in a wet suit. Eric is of the opinion that if it doesn't involve a ball, it isn't a sport … although I've taught him a few athletic moves that might change his mind." She flashed a wicked grin.

"Yikes! Too much information!" Jane sputtered, laughing.

"Kayaking god," Flory intoned quietly, as Jake approached. Flory had been dating Mark Co for two years, and they got along better than most couples Jane knew. But he was working today and wouldn't arrive 'til evening, and as Flory said, just because she had a boyfriend didn't mean she was blind.

"Hey, Jane," Jake said, shifting a little awkwardly as he stood above the girls' beach blanket, a blush creeping through the tan on his face. Jane breathed again. He was human after all, just like she'd remembered.

Their first date had gone well—he'd bought them hot cocoa from Hilltop Grocery & Café and they'd walked around Elfin Lake after school. She spotted a northern flicker mining an old fir tree stump for insects, and recognized the calls of starlings, Steller's jays, and American robins—something she couldn't have done even a month ago. She was stumped by a strange "meep-meep" until she realized it was Jake, crouched behind a tree, imitating the Roadrunner. He made them both laugh, and laughing had made them relax.

He asked her a million questions about the day of the oil spill, and complimented her over and over again on her courage in jumping into the Inlet and speaking out against the oil company. He called her a hero. Jane tried to make him understand that it had just happened, that the words had just tumbled out, and he seemed to realize that he'd made her uncomfortable. He stopped walking and turned to face her, took her hand, looked intently into her eyes and said, "Okay, you're *my* hero, then."

Blushing furiously, she smiled back at him and wondered when exactly she'd agreed to the emotional roller-coaster ride of the past few days. She quickly changed the subject, asking him about the upcoming basketball game against South Slope, and was relieved when he became engrossed in the subject and left the oil spill behind. He'd hugged her goodbye, which was also a huge relief—her life was already moving too fast as it was. But she knew it was only a matter of time before her first kiss, and she was giddy at the thought that it would be with Jake Harbinsale.

"Hey," she answered him now, "how are you..." Little Bobby Harbinsale came running up behind his older brother and threw a bucket of water at his head. At four feet tall, the ten-year-old's aim fell short and the cold lake water drenched the girls instead. Flory screamed, Bobby ran away howling with laughter and Jake swung around just in time to grab a handful of empty air.

"Oh, man, I'm so sorry," Jake apologized, bending to help towel up the mess until he realized he was crouched in the middle of a blanket with three bikini-clad girls. He stood up again, embarrassed. "My mom always says god makes 'em cute so you don't kill 'em, but I swear if I catch that kid alone this weekend…" He trailed off, grinning at Jane.

"Listen, the real reason I came over here was to ask you over for dinner before we head to the dance," Jake said, looking only at Jane as the others packed up their soaked belongings. "My dad hauled the barbecue out of the shed this morning and my mom's been cooking up a storm."

Jane looked quickly over at Amy. There likely wouldn't be too many more warm weekends this year, and she'd counted on a big family dinner with the MacGillivrays and her two best friends. She also felt a little awkward that Jake hadn't included her friends in his invitation.

"You have our permission to separate the three of us just this once," Amy answered, her face and voice completely serious. "But on one condition."

"Oh?" Jake asked, unsure how to take this challenge. "And what's that?"

Amy snuck a wink at Flory before turning an innocent face to Jake: "You have to save at least one dance tonight for Flory and me. Each."

"Done!" Jake smiled, looking relieved. "So, six o'clock? Last cabin on Driftwood Street, red door." Jane nodded, holding his gaze and smiling. He'd just undergone the Amy MacGillivray Test of Manhood and passed with flying colors. Her friends liked him, he'd invited her to meet his family, and she was going to the Harvest Dance with him tonight. If this year got any better, she thought, she might just lift off and float away.

As Jake sauntered down the dirt path toward the Harbinsale cabin, rowing jacket tied low over his hips, Flory turned to Jane and Amy, her face serious and her round, black eyes wide. "Dancing god," she whispered reverently. Amy bit her lip and glanced over at Jane, signaling her with a look. In unison, Amy grabbed Flory's ankles and Jane held her arms, and together they ran down the dock and tossed the squealing girl into the lake.

12
ONCE UPON A TIME

ONCE UPON A TIME, the Rays, the MacGillivrays, and the Moraleses had all owned cabins on Cultus Lake. Now, only the MacGillivrays' remained. The other two cabins were still there, of course, but other families owned them and rented them out, and now their children built sandcastles and flew paper kites and ran in and out of the deck doors as Jane and Flory had done in the past. Mr. and Mrs. Morales sold theirs when the real estate market boomed, and Jane's parents sold at a loss when their own fortunes tumbled. Knowing what their Cultus summers and weekends together meant to the three best friends, Mr. and Mrs. MacGillivray made it clear that the last remaining cabin belonged to all of them, squeezing in bunk beds and a bigger dining table without giving it a second thought.

The girls' parents had gone to university together in the 1980s, and the three families' photo albums looked almost like copies of one another. Pictures of protest marches, political demonstrations, and late-night cafés gave way to wedding photos, and then baby pictures, and then page after page of the three inseparable friends, playing dress-up, putting on shows, riding bikes, selling lemonade. The backdrop was always a lake—either Elfin or Cultus—and the supporting cast included Amy's older brother Mike, Flory's two younger sisters, Nikki and Maria, and a coterie of animal companions who willingly put up with the costumes and wagon rides for a chance to be part of the play.

The MacGillivrays' yellow and white bungalow was as small as they come. When you opened the front door, you looked straight through the cabin to the lake. It was a matter of maybe twenty steps from the front door to the sliding glass doors at the back. To the left of the entrance was the bathroom, and to the right, the bedroom the girls shared, followed by the master bedroom. The kitchen opened into the dining area, which in turn opened into the living room and hearth. The glass doors let onto a small porch, and a single step down put you on the grassy southwest shore of Cultus Lake.

Malcolm and Marion MacGillivray had always regretted missing out on the hippie era of the 1960s and early '70s, and in an imagined sense of nostalgia decorated the cabin in true psychedelic style: lava lamps and fiber optic fountain lights throughout, a curtain of cowrie shell beads over the girls' bedroom door, orange and brown shag carpet, an orange Naugahyde couch, and a fake bearskin rug in front of the fireplace. In almost twenty years, not a thing had changed.

Amy swept the beads aside and walked in on Jane and Flory laying their clothes out for the Harvest Dance that night. "Yeow! Sexy!" Flory twirled around between the bunk beds holding up a slender, black, one-shouldered sheath dress. "Flory, I swear you're skinnier than ever. Sorry, *slimmer*. I'm going to be a wallflower next to you two." She pulled a teal green tunic embroidered with gold thread and denim capris from the closet and reached for the iron.

"Whatever!" Jane laughed. At five foot nothing, with generous curves, prominent features, and a mass of unruly red curls, Amy wasn't fashion-model pretty. But she was invariably surrounded by a group of guys, all happy to take turns taking her out. She made people laugh, and she had a way of turning even homework and chores into adventures. Wallflower was out of the question. More likely belle of the ball.

Jane held the butter yellow halter dress up to her lanky runner's frame and smiled at the silver screen star she saw gazing back at her from the full-length mirror. The color suited her dark hair and olive skin, and brought out the deep blue of her eyes. Made of a soft, flowing fabric, the dress was fitted to the waist, flaring out into a full skirt. She'd bought it for $15 at Legends, one of her favorite second-hand shops, along with a cream-colored beaded capelet, and the owner had told her they were vintage 1960s. The dress made her feel considerably older than sixteen, and she wondered what Jake would think when he saw her in it.

"Mike's arriving tonight," Amy said casually without looking up from her ironing. "He asked me on the phone if you were going to be here, Jane, and said he had something he wanted to ask you." Amy's older brother Mike had spent the summer working on an organic farm, and they'd all missed him. Jane realized suddenly that she hadn't even spotted him in the halls since school had started, and she was glad to hear they'd have a chance to catch up this weekend.

"Probably wants to tease me about being on TV," Jane guessed, glancing at her watch.

"Mmph," Amy mumbled. "Maybe."

"Hey, it's getting close to six! I've got to get going! I'll come back here after dinner to change, and I'll meet you guys there, okay?"

"Wait up, we'll come with you," Flory answered. "Amy's mom wants us to pick stuff up for dinner."

At Logan's Market, they filled a basket with lettuce, cucumber, and tomatoes for a salad, carrots, onions, celery, plum tomatoes, and black olives for spaghetti sauce, a loaf of garlic bread, and bananas, mini marshmallows, and chocolate chips to roast together in foil packets for dessert.

Outside the store, Amy popped a quarter into the gumball machine and turned the knob while Jane and Flory shook the machine. Four polished orbs rolled out of the chute. "Not bad," Amy nodded approvingly. "I'll save the blue one for Mike." She glanced over at the mechanical race car, its red paint faded with sun and age, and then at Jane: "Got time for a ride?"

"Of course!" They all climbed on and Jane slid a quarter into the slot. Flory squealed as the little car lurched forward. It pitched backward and then leapt forward again, roughly imitating the movement of an arthritic jumping horse. Amy got the giggles, and soon her face was streaming with tears. Jane laughed at Amy's laugh, and soon the three of them were howling. Suddenly the car started to shimmy, and a loud rattle almost drowned out the girls' laughter. The car stopped in mid-lurch, leapt to life again for a few seconds, and then died.

"Oh my god, we've killed it! We're too fat!" Flory cried.

"No, Flory," Amy answered, wiping her eyes. "We're too old."

"I'd love to stick around, but I've got a barbecue to get to," Jane interjected, half wishing she were going to the MacGillivray dinner instead. "You guys'd better let Mr. Logan know about this," she said, nodding toward the car.

Amy looked aghast. Flory rolled her eyes. "I'll do it," she said, marching back into the store. Amy looked at Jane and grinned. "Knock 'em dead, girl!"

13

JANE MEETS THE HARBINSALES

R AND HARBINSALE STOOD CHOKING on a piece of rare barbecued steak and for a moment Jane thought she was going to have to perform the Heimlich maneuver. Randy Junior saved her from the decision by reaching in front of his father and shaking Jane's hand. His eyes locked on hers as he said, "You're certainly looking more...mature since the last time we saw you, Jane!" He held her hand longer than he needed to, and Jane finally had to pull it away. He was so much like Jake, and yet somehow more of everything—older, taller, bigger, stronger, more confident... Cocky was more like it, she thought. He had a way of seeming to take up all the space, even out here in the back yard, and Jane wondered if Jake felt that way about him, too. At the moment, he seemed to be shooting his father some sort of meaningful look.

Reasonably recovered, Rand Senior shook her hand, and Jane watched him turn on the charm she'd heard talk of for years, as though he were flipping a switch. "So *you're* the new girlfriend we've been hearing so much about! Funny, I guess Jake never mentioned your name." He smiled broadly at his middle son, but there was steel in his eyes. It was starting to feel like a Wimbledon match with all the strange looks passing back and forth, and Jane was relieved when Mrs. Harbinsale called them all in to the dining table.

"Jane's the one who was on TV after that oil spill," Jake said, after Donna Lise had finished saying a quick grace. "Why don't you tell everybody how you rescued that bird, Jane?" Shyly at first, but soon warming to the now-familiar story, Jane began to tell the Harbinsale family about her half-marathon training, sighting the scoter, the scene at the UWRC, and the television interview that had ended up on national news. After a few minutes, she realized that Mr. and Mrs. Harbinsale and Randy Jr. were just picking at their food, and she quickly turned to Jake to see if he could provide her with a clue to whether she'd said or done something wrong. But Jake was busy slicing through steak and heaping his plate with mashed potatoes, a small smile on his face. Bobby was no help either; he'd turned his jellied salad into an obstacle course and was driving a pickled beet through it, complete with sound effects.

She shook her head to try and clear it, and her story trickled to an anticlimactic end. "More devilled eggs, dear?" Mrs. Harbinsale was suddenly at her side with platter and spoon. In some part of her mind, Jane registered her expensive pastel linen pant suit and loafers, her perfectly coiffed blonde hair, and elegant, manicured hands. But what grabbed her attention was the fact that those hands were shaking. Something was really wrong, and Jane wracked her memory for anything she'd said that could have offended Jake's family. She had the odd sensation of being at the dinner table with her mom, where she'd stopped saying anything at all just to be safe, and recalled how good it had felt to be talking so easily since the day of the oil spill. She'd thought that was a good thing, but now she wasn't so sure.

"I took the Sea-Doo out for a spin on the lake this afternoon," Randy Jr. said, breaking the tension. "Greg Davison and I took turns seeing who could scare the most ducks into the air at one time. I won!" Jane's appetite, already waning, vanished. "I think Greg clipped a couple of 'em, but it was hard to tell. They'll be fine, I'm sure. It's so crowded on that damn lake now. And it's not as if they're an endangered species!" He laughed at his own unquestionable logic. "Oh, and hey dad, you gotta get that thing looked at. It's leaking motor oil like a sonofabitch."

"They're alive, you know," Jane blurted out before she could stop herself. "They have feelings and families and things they want to do besides getting out of *your* way, and they can suffer." She could hear her voice rising, and the two Randys were staring at her as if she were a space alien. But she couldn't stop. "You can't go around terrorizing them or running them down for *fun*, as if they're bowling pins or buoys." She was shaking now herself. "They're *alive*."

"Can I get you some lemon chiffon cake, Jane?" Mrs. Harbinsale asked without missing a beat. As if she hadn't said a word.

"Me, please!" Bobby yelled.

"Me, too, mom," Randy Jr. said, holding out his side plate.

"Me three, honey!" Rand turned his smile on his wife.

"No thanks, Mrs. Harbinsale," Jane said miserably.

"Actually, the dance has already started. Would you guys mind if we left you with the dishes?" Jane saw that Jake could turn on the Harbinsale charm, too, when he wanted to. On automatic pilot, she shook hands and thanked Jake's mom, and made it out to the street before bursting into tears.

"I'm so sorry, Jake! I don't know what I said wrong but I obviously upset your family and I'm so embarrassed but I just couldn't seem to stop what I was saying and maybe Randy was just joking and your mom was just trying to be nice but ....." Jake took her by the shoulders and kissed her, quieting her sobs and starting her shaking again.

"Jane, don't cry," he said quietly, smoothing her hair away from her face. "You were great. You didn't do anything wrong. You said what you needed to say, which just happened to be some stuff my jerk of a brother needed to hear. I'm proud of you." He was holding her tightly now, and whispering into her ear. "Come dance with me."

Jane was giddy with his kiss, and with his words. She held his hand tightly as they walked toward the MacGillivray cabin. She was amazed. He was proud of her, and thought what she'd said at dinner was right, even though that put his family in the wrong. It never occurred to her to wonder why he'd let her fight the battle with his family alone.

14

THE BUTTERFLY EFFECT

AS SOON AS JANE'S EYES ADJUSTED to the dim light, she spotted Amy and Flory at the refreshment counter, waving like semaphore flagsmen. Eric Fabbro towered above Amy and gazed adoringly at her as he passed her a tumbler of punch. Flory's boyfriend Mark had arrived just in time for the dance, and stood behind her with his arms wrapped around her waist. Jane gave her a discreet thumbs-up and Flory returned the signal.

Changing into her dancing clothes had helped her shake off the disastrous dinner with the Harbinsales, and the look on Jake's face when she emerged from the bedroom in the yellow dress had made her forget all about it. She blushed again, remembering how his voice had broken and he'd stuttered a few incoherent words before shutting his mouth and just staring.

Jake took her hand and they made their way through the crowded room, stopping to say hi to local neighbors and friends Jane had known all her life.

The Cultus Community Hall was the cultural center—such as it was—of the little lakeside town, and the Saturday night dances were a highlight for the regulars. On the small raised stage at the far end of the room, The Cult-us were winding down a Shania Twain song. Women and men in their forties and fifties, The Cult-us jammed and rehearsed together all year round, covering well-known country tunes and pop songs from the '60s through to the present day that everybody could dance to. At some point tonight, they'd lead the whole crowd in a line dance, but just now, they were launching into a kick-ass rendition of Aretha Franklin's "Rescue Me."

"Hey, Jane, they're playing your song!" Jake smiled and tugged at her hand.

"Her scoter's song, you mean," Amy countered, one eyebrow raised.

"Right, yeah. Okay, sweetie, let's dance!" Jake and Jane disappeared into the throng.

"'Sweetie! Honey! Baby!' Well, aren't things progressing nicely!" Amy raised her punch glass and clinked it against Flory's. "I just hope he remembers our bargain." She took a long draft of punch, remembering Eric's presence just in time to stop herself from belching.

Jake kept Jane out on the floor for every dance, all evening long, until she laughingly reminded him that he owed Amy and Flory each a dance, too. They'd had no shortage of partners themselves, but Jake kept his promise and danced with each one. Then the music changed and slowed, and he turned back to Jane, holding out a hand, his head tilted a little to one side and a crooked smile softening his face. "Last dance," he said. She stepped forward, and folded herself into his arms.

In the middle of the dance, he pulled away from her slightly, and she looked up to find him gazing down at her, his face alight with a look she was learning to recognize. Her heart started to pound. "There's something I'd like to do over again, now that you're smiling," he said. He kissed her, softly, cupping her face in his hands, and Jane could have sworn that, just for an instant, the band stopped playing.

And then he was holding her and they were dancing and the music was playing and the ceiling fans were spinning and Amy and Flory were whirling past her in the arms of their partners, eyes closed and dreamy smiles playing across their faces. Something caused her to turn and look at the entrance to the Hall, and the figure she saw silhouetted there in the doorway made her do a double-take.

"What?" Jake whispered in her ear.

"Nothing," she answered, and rested her head against his shoulder. As soon as she'd looked over, the figure had disappeared, as though he'd been watching her and hadn't wanted to be seen. He. Who? Someone familiar, someone who reminded her somehow of home, of Elfin Lake, someone almost like family, but a stranger, with his shock of long, wavy hair and solid, powerful presence. He'd turned her head like a magnet. If he was even real, she thought, tightening her arms around Jake's very real waist.

The song ended, the lights came up, and people started to gather their children and their belongings and head toward the doors. "C'mon," Jake said, "I'll walk you home."

Jane tiptoed past the two bedrooms and straight into the kitchen, hunting for leftovers. She'd hardly touched her dinner at the Harbinsales', and had had nothing but fruit punch for the past four hours. Swinging the fridge door wide, she gasped as the light it threw revealed a sleeping figure on the couch. For a split second, she thought she was dreaming. It was her silhouetted man from the dance! Then she recognized him and had to stifle a laugh; it was just Mike, Amy's older brother. She'd forgotten he was supposed to show up tonight.

He groaned and rolled over to face her, squinting

in the light. "For the love of all things holy, woman, would you shut the ... Oh! ... Jane! ... It's you!" He sat bolt upright, looked down quickly as if to make sure he was wearing something (Jane put a hand to her mouth to stop herself from laughing; she'd seen those faded plaid boxers and that threadbare Henley pullover way too many times), then put his fists to his eyes to rub the sleep away.

He's changed, she thought. He'd let his hair grow, for one thing, but it wasn't just that. He looked older, not like the kid in all her photo albums, but more like ... what? Himself, is what she'd been thinking. More like who he was.

"You haven't changed," he said, when he could see straight. She frowned. Sure, they hadn't seen one another since June. And ordinarily, she saw him every weekend at Cultus during the summer, or at the MacGillivray place during the week, but then he'd found the job on Whole Earth Organic Farms, and somehow school had started up again without their paths crossing, and so for the first time in their lives, months had gone by. Surely she'd grown up a little, too.

"Your dress, I mean," he added, comprehending the look on her face. He smiled, not quite meeting her eyes. "You were wearing it at the dance. I really ... it suits you," he finished quietly.

So it *was* him she'd glimpsed standing in the Community Hall doorway! Suddenly she realized he'd seen her kissing Jake, and she felt her face grow hot. She was glad of the darkness of the room. This was the guy who'd spent practically his entire life teasing her—about her haircuts, her "antique" outfits, as he called her vintage clothes, her purple bicycle, her cats, the books she read, the way she ran—about everything. But here he was, in possession of the best reason yet to tease the daylights out of her, and instead he was complimenting her! Well, almost. As close as any of the MacGillivray clan ever got to a compliment. He *has* changed, she thought. Why did *everything* seem to be changing right now?

She seated herself on the arm of the couch a little distance from Mike, and stared out at the lake, the ins and outs of its shoreline and the rippling patterns on its silver-indigo surface as familiar as the palm of her own hand. Out of the corner of her eye, she watched Mike as he gazed out at the same scene, and knew that the memories she had of childhood summers spent here were his as well. Those, at least, nothing could change.

"Ame said you had something to ask me," she said, suddenly remembering. Mike turned his head and stared at her, and for a brief moment she was afraid he was going to compliment her again. He narrowed his eyes, and his mouth tightened a little, as though he were trying to make a decision about something.

"Nope," he finally said, shaking his head slowly. "Crazy sister of mine, so often wrong," he joked. Jane managed a smile, thinking, this is different too, this pretending and subtext and trying to read between the lines. She knew Amy hadn't been mistaken, but she also knew instinctively that pressing Mike now wouldn't be a good idea. She just wasn't sure why.

"Something to *tell* you, though." He looked up at her intently. "Can you keep a secret?" She nodded, thinking that this was a first.

"This is going to be my last year of school."

Jane laughed, not understanding. "This *is* your last year of school, Mike. You graduate next June. I hate to tell you this, but your secret's already out!"

But he startled her by reaching across the couch and gripping one of her hands in his. "Right, and I'm going to university to study engineering just like everybody expects ... except I'm not."

Jane squeezed his hand. "What do you mean? It's what you've always wanted to do! You're so good at building things and figuring out how stuff works and ... and making things out of nothing. What would you do instead?"

"All those things," he answered, "except on a farm."

"Ohhh!" she breathed, finally beginning to understand. "You liked it that much?"

"Jane, it was *magic*. From planting the seeds in the spring, to being part of the team that protects the seedlings and then tending the young shoots, and finally the harvest of the past weeks. And everything natural, the way farming used to be. I've never been part of anything like it." His eyes shone as he described his summer to her, and Jane felt herself get caught up in his excitement. *He feels about farming the same way I do about animals*, she realized.

"We're destroying our food supply on this planet, Jane, but in just a few months I realized that even one person, even little old me, could change that." He pulled his hand back gently and looked away. "I guess it really hit home when I saw you on TV."

"Me?" she squeaked. "You're ditching university and risking being disowned by the MacGillivray clan because of *me*?"

He chuckled softly. "Yeah, I'm really going to have to time *that* conversation well, huh?" His face grew serious. "Jane, have you heard of the butterfly effect?" She shook her head. "It's related to chaos theory and fractals and stuff, and the basic premise is that when a butterfly flutters its wings in one part of the world, it can eventually cause a hurricane in another." He got that odd, complimenting look on his face again, and Jane noticed it seemed to have a direct effect on her breathing. "You're like that butterfly, Jane, and the difference you've made to me is just one of the aftershocks. The real storm is what you're trying to do with the oil company, and for the animals. You've really started something, Jane Ray."

Jane didn't know what to think about Mike's words, let alone what to say. It seemed to her like he was talking about someone else—some grown up who wore expensive clothes and always knew the right thing to say and could convince CEOs and government officials to come around to her infallible way of thinking. Not a mud-soaked sixteen-year-old who'd become furious over a duck and opened her mouth before she could think twice.

Mike had turned back to the windows, and was watching a pale white moth flutter blindly around the porch light. "It's not easy, what you're trying to do." She could barely hear him. "Just ... just be careful."

He turned again, the seriousness replaced by a challenging grin. "How about a run tomorrow morning?" She grinned back, relieved to be on familiar ground again. Mike had run the Holiday Half last year, and had offered to help her train if she ever decided to try it herself.

"You're on! Those lazy-bum friends of mine gave me strict orders not to wake them up early tomorrow. Said tonight wore them out."

"Since when does slow-dancing count as a workout?" he scoffed. "How does 7:00 a.m. sound?"

She groaned. "Make it 7:30."

"As you wish, princess, but we'll do a little hill training as punishment, then, hmm?"

"Good*night*, Mac!" She stood up and headed to the bedrooms. Mac. She hadn't called him that since they were kids. She could hear him chuckling at the name. "Good luck telling your parents about your change of plans. Somehow, I think they'll understand."

"Thanks," he grinned. "'Night, Butterfly."

Still smiling, she stepped through the bead curtain without looking back, and didn't see him stare after her for another ten minutes before finally lying down and falling back to sleep.

15

FLIGHT OR FIGHT

*Flight or fight: In nature, an animal who feels threat-
ened typically experiences a "flight or fight" response. The
response is instinctive, controlled by the autonomic nervous
system, and consists physiologically of an increase in heart
rate, dilated pupils, increased blood pressure and muscular
tension, respiration rate, and cardiac output. The animal
is preparing to defend itself against the threat, either by
running away (flight; passive) or by meeting aggression
with aggression and standing its ground (fight; active).*

— from Flory's Files

THE CHILL MORNING AIR smelled of rain, and
damp, rotting leaves, and rush-hour exhaust. Jane
spotted the lights of the Care Center winking through
the trees around the last bend in the road, and despite
the cold, she felt another few drops of sweat slither
down her back, gluing her shirt to her body in a clammy
mass. It was Thursday, 7:52. She was about to start her
first shift as a new volunteer at the Urban Wildlife Rescue
Center. And she couldn't remember a thing.

This morning when her alarm had gone off, she'd sat up in bed clutching her stomach, her mind a blank. *I'll call in sick*, she thought. *I'll go next week instead. I need to study the manual some more.*

But she knew she'd only feel worse next week, and she knew she wasn't really sick. She was scared. Sucking in a deep breath, she swung open the door.

"Morning, Jane!" Evie called from the exam room, where she was drawing up medications. "Have you and Anthony already met?" Anthony was talking on the phone, winking, and giving her the peace sign all at once. "Avis has started on the outside animals, and Anthony will give her a hand once the phones quiet down. Can I assign you to feed and clean the inside animals with Katrina?"

Katrina D'Angelo was a tall, athletic grade twelve girl whom Jane recognized from Cedar's Ridge High. Jane watched her wrap and remove birds from their cages, and quickly fell into step behind her, cleaning cages whenever an animal was out for weighing or medicating, so that it didn't have to be disturbed twice. As she began to relax, bit by bit the training started to come back. She timed her meal-making to coincide with Avis's absences from the kitchen, and worked with Katrina in the care room whenever Avis came inside. *The old bat didn't even say hello*, Jane thought. *Hmph. Just as well.*

"So, do you have a boyfriend?" the older girl asked, sweeping her shoulder-length blonde hair off her face.

"Oh, uh, yeah." Jane smiled shyly.

"Uh-huh … and he is …" Katrina prompted.

"Oh! Jake Harbinsale, from Cedar's Ridge. He plays basketball, and …"

"Jake Harbinsale! Of course I know who *he* is. Nice catch, girl!" Jane realized she had secured Katrina's instant approval. Or at least, her boyfriend had.

"I dated Cal Clarkson last year, but I broke up with him over the summer. He got kind of boring, you know? No car, so we could never go anywhere. We just hung out at the lake all the time. Yawn!" Jane couldn't imagine anywhere she'd rather be than the lake, but she kept silent.

"But! My latest target just asked me out this week! Do you know Mike MacGillivray?"

Jane swung around, nearly knocking a tray of dirty dishes to the ground. Mike? With Katrina D'Angelo? She wouldn't have put the two of them together in a million years.

"Um, yeah. His sister Amy is one of my best friends," she finally answered.

"Oh, right! Funny little Amy. Anyway, Mike's really got it going on. He's an amazing soccer player, and next year he's going to university to become an engineer! Total brainiac. I think we click because I remind him not to take life too seriously." Jane suppressed a snort. Mike, serious. That was good. She'd have to tell Amy that one. *I guess he hasn't managed to tell the family yet about his change in career plans,* she thought. *Or his new girlfriend.*

"Jane, want to give me a hand with the scaup?" Evie was removing the cover from the net-bottomed floor pen. "He has to be tube-fed." Jane checked the clock as she followed Evie to the exam room—it said 10:45.

"Evie, is that clock right?"

"Time flies when you're knee-deep in you know what, eh?" Evie grinned.

She placed the wrapped bird on the examining table. "I'll hold, you feed." She nodded at a long, supple tube attached to a syringe filled with fish slurry, a pinkish mixture of blended salmon and water, and then propped open the scaup's bill with her fingers. "That small opening you see in the throat is called the glottis, and it leads to the lungs. You put the tube down there by accident and he'll aspirate the mixture and die. You want to slide the tube in just beside the glottis, and keep easing it in until it won't go any further. Excellent! Now slowly … *slowly* squeeze the tube mixture out, and keep watch on his throat. If he starts to regurgitate it, pinch off the tube, pull it out quickly and get out of the way."

"Why can't you give him solid fish and protein mix like the other water birds?" Jane asked, her eyes locked on the scaup she'd come secretly to think of as Scotty.

"When he was oiled, his waterproofing was all but destroyed," Evie replied. "He'll get it back over time, but meanwhile, if he slapped his wing into his food dish and got fish oil on his feathers, we'd be back at square one. We're tube-feeding all the oil spill birds right now, even the ones outside."

Once the syringe was empty, Evie showed Jane how to remove the tube and they waited a few minutes to make sure the scaup was going to keep the food down. "So, Daniel tells me you were heading off to write an email to SeaKing the other day," Evie said nonchalantly. Jane could see by her eyes, though, that she was keen to know what had come of it.

She pulled a piece of letterhead from her pocket. "*Dear Ms. Ray,*" she read. "*Thank you for your interest in SeaKing Shipping Pacific. The recent canola spill was an unfortunate accident, but while SeaKing regrets any environmental impact this event may have caused, we would also like to remind our shareholders as well as members of the public that the corporation bears no direct responsibility for this incident.*

We have done everything possible to assist with the clean-up process, and are undergoing a standard investigation procedure in order to satisfy industry protocol. Again, we are taking proactive steps to minimize the impact of the accident, and value our partnerships with those community groups involved in doing the same.

Thank you again.

Sincerely,
Alan Coyne, CEO
SeaKing Shipping Pacific"

"Partnerships my ass!" Evie sputtered. "Sorry, Jane. I shouldn't talk like that. But the reality is, we haven't heard a single word from those people since the day of the spill, let alone seen that donation they promised. That form letter is a load of crap. And what burns my ... *butt* is that it was one of their own who called in the tip! Somebody there has a conscience, but apparently it's not upper management." She shook her head, not looking at Jane. "Our only hope now is that investigation. If it turns out they've been negligent, they'll be forced to pay for cleanup and animal rehabilitation. But if, for some reason, the investigator can't prove it, I can't see them covering any of these costs out of the goodness of their hearts."

Evie left the exam room, carrying the scaup, and Jane stood alone, taking in the import of what she'd said. It was obvious to her that the UWRC ran on one part cash and three parts passion, and that any extra expenditures could hurt the organization badly. The costs of rescuing and rehabilitating the birds caught in the canola spill stretched the little Center past its limits, and if SeaKing didn't own up to its role in the mess, something here would snap. Well, if an email didn't get their attention, maybe a formal letter would. She was composing it in her mind when Avis poked her head into the room.

"I'm putting the coffee on now. I'll see you in the lunchroom in ten minutes." She bustled out the front door before Jane had the chance to respond.

Oh god, what had she done? Not rinsed some of her dirty dishes? Put the black oil sunflower seeds back where the striped ones belonged? She racked her brains trying to figure out what mistake had caused Avis to single her out for punishment. And coffee? What had she meant about coffee?

Ten minutes later, she stepped into the lunchroom in the basement of the old house, determined not to let the old biddy intimidate her, and found Avis seated in one of the tattered chairs, two steaming mugs of coffee and a plate of homemade cookies in front of her on the table. "Cream and sugar?" the older woman inquired brightly.

"Oh! Uh, cream please. And thanks." Jane

wondered if the snack was supposed to soften the blow of whatever came next. But there was no *next*. There was just the ticking of the clock on the wall, the thick, cozy smell of coffee, and Avis's fresh-baked peanut and raisin cookies.

After a few minutes, Jane cleared her throat. "So, were you really in the Navy?"

"World War II. Women's Royal Canadian Naval Service. Known as the Wrens. I was stationed at St. Hyacinthe in Quebec to learn the semaphore flags and Morse code, and then in Halifax where I worked in the signal tower. It was quite an adventure, I'll tell you. Met my first husband there!" For the first time since Jane had met her, Avis smiled, and all of a sudden Jane could see the young woman in uniform, not much older than herself. Trying to do the right thing in a difficult time.

"Evie tells me you've taken quite an interest in this oil spill," Avis said.

"It's what brought me here," Jane answered simply, "and it got me on the news because I couldn't keep my mouth shut."

"There's a time and a place to keep your mouth shut, but an oil spill isn't it," Avis said tersely. "Evie and Daniel and Anthony and the staff don't have time to take on the oil companies—they're too busy cleaning up after them! But somebody needs to.

Somebody needs to tell the truth about lax standards and shoddy inspection practices and lack of understanding about the long-term results of these spills. It's got to stop."

"Did you come here because of an oil spill?" Jane asked her.

Avis shook her head. "I came here fifteen years ago because I love birds. I love their songs and their shapes and the different ways they move in flight, their mating rituals, and the racket of them all in the spring, when the babies are born and calling for food. I *love* them. And I can see now that little by little we are destroying their world." She'd been gazing out the kitchen window to the hummingbird garden, but now she turned and looked directly at Jane.

"I watched the devastation of the Exxon Valdez spill on my living room television helpless to do anything about it. So I got my hands dirty with the last two canola spills here. My husband George and I went to Spain in 2002 to volunteer with the cleanup operations there. I tell you, if there's such a thing as hell, that was it. Miles of blackened shores, thick with sludge, and thousands of animals caught, nowhere to go to get away, dying in our hands before we could reach them, dying before we ever even found them. It was exhausting, physically and emotionally. I don't think I could do it again."

Avis stood up abruptly and went to the coffee pot to refill her mug. Back at the table, she picked up the day's newspaper and began to flip through it. *Conversation over,* Jane thought. She understood why.

Suddenly Avis let out a stream of words Jane had never heard from a woman her age. "How on god's green earth did they manage to pull the wool ... This *has* to be a cover-up! But how?"

"What? What is it?" Jane had a terrible feeling she knew exactly what it was. Avis slid the newspaper across the table, and there, buried at the back of section B, was the short article: *SeaKing cleared of blame for spill.*

A formal investigation into the canola spill that took place in the early hours of October 17 has exonerated SeaKing Shipping Pacific of any legal responsibility for the incident. Independent investigators found evidence that the company's pipeline was punctured by a sharp object, such as a rock or an anchor, and was not worn or corroded as earlier allegations had suggested. This leaves SeaKing with no obligation to cover the costs of cleanup or wildlife rehabilitation, costs that could reach as high as half a million dollars. Neither Federal nor Provincial representatives have indicated whether they will pay any portion of those costs, since they now have no way of recovering any money from SeaKing Shipping. SeaKing loads the familiar cooking oil onto cargo ships at a rate of 400 tonnes per hour, and an estimated 50 tonnes—or 200,000 gallons—leaked into Burrard Inlet. SeaKing employees detected the spill within minutes, shutting off the pumps. The tide dispersed the oil west through the Inlet toward open waters and the winter nesting grounds of several species of migratory waterfowl. The Urban Wildlife Rescue Center and the Cedar's Ridge SPCA have headed up animal rescue operations, at significant cost to themselves. Both organizations were counting on this investigation to hold SeaKing financially responsible. But they will now have to rely on the corporation's willingness to make a donation, something SeaKing promised earlier to do. In the past, oil spill cleanup was provided at no charge by the Canadian Coast Guard but, due to the increasing number and scale of spills, is now offered only by private companies. Those responsible for spills will often voluntarily pay to secure the services of one of these cleanup companies but SeaKing did not do so.

Avis stood abruptly and threw the coffee mugs into the sink with a clatter, scrubbing them 'til Jane thought they'd crumble in her hands. She clipped the article from the page, thanked Avis for the coffee and cookies, and turned to go. Then she looked back at the older woman, military posture abandoned as she slumped low over the sink. "I'm going to show this to Evie," she said. "She needs to know."

Slowly, Avis nodded. "So that's the end of that story, I suppose."

Jane gazed back at the bright blue eyes that sparked with life every time Avis talked about birds. "No," she answered. "Not yet. I'm going to write another letter."

16
NOT A WORD

WAYDE COYNE KEPT HIS EYES ON BELINDA and Mason as they stood over him at his desk, and slowly reached down to slide his bottom drawer shut. He was pretty sure they hadn't spotted the guacamole tortilla chips or the three-bean dip, and he just hoped Belinda's perfume covered up that beany smell. He saw her crinkle up her nose, and had a feeling he knew what she was thinking. He blushed.

"Uncle Al … er … Mr. Coyne has cancelled all his meetings again this week," he stammered. "I'd be happy to pass the information along to him for you, though."

Mason sighed, looking frustrated. Geeky little self-important twerp, Wayde thought. Wayde had always pegged him for the type that put charitable gifts above the bottom line. Takes one to know one, he supposed, reminding himself of the time he'd donated their entire fourth-quarter profits to a cottage-industry start-up program for street people that had turned out to be a scam. Well, Wayde was looking after his uncle now, and this wasn't the time to be leaking cash to everybody and his dog.

"Just tell him …" Mason started. "I mean, if you would please just let him know that even though the insurance settlement wasn't as high as we'd hoped, there's still room in the budget for the donations we promised to the UWRC and the SPCA."

"But no dog and pony show this time!" Belinda snapped, cracking her gum for emphasis. "I've had it up to my C-cups dealing with the media over this spill. No media releases, no press conference, no nothing. And then maybe we can all just forget about this and get on with our lives!"

Wayde smiled up at her, and reached out to take the spreadsheet Mason offered. As he folded it in thirds and slipped it into an envelope, he said quietly, almost as if to himself, "Not a word."

17
JAKE'S GIFT

EVERY THURSDAY AFTERNOON for the next several weeks, Jane went home from school, or to the Shack, to Jake's place, or to a sheltered spot along the shore of Elfin Lake and wrote a letter to Alan Coyne, CEO, SeaKing Shipping Pacific. *My new pen pal*, she joked to Jake. She wrote about the UWRC staff and volunteers she'd met, about Scotty growing strong enough to be moved outside, about the recovery and release of three of Sadie's teals, about the numbers of birds that had come in, both alive and dead, and the number that now survived. She wrote about what it took to help just one bird recover from being oiled—in time and food and individual care, and in money. She told this man she'd never met what it felt like to release a bird back to the wild, and she asked him to make good on his promise to donate.

For the first couple of weeks, she received letters back on SeaKing stationery. She tore each one open in excitement, hoping they contained news of a donation, or even a check she could deliver to the UWRC herself. The first, though, was a duplicate of the form letter she'd read to Evie. The second was a new form letter, obviously written after the investigation, that made it clear the canola spill was no longer of any concern whatsoever to SeaKing Shipping. After that, she received no response at all.

Toward the end of November, Jake encouraged her to try calling the CEO directly. "Pick up the phone," he said. "That way they can't ignore you."

She called every day for five days. It made her terribly nervous to imagine herself talking to the CEO, and her hands trembled each time as she punched in the numbers. Until the fifth call, when she realized she was never going to get through to Alan Coyne. "I'm sorry," his receptionist answered in the same detached tone each time, "Mr. Coyne is in a meeting. May I take a message?"

"Yes!" she blurted out. "Tell him that's one damn long meeting!" She slammed down the phone. She turned around to find Jake grinning at her from the couch, where Sweet Pea and Minnie were vying for his affections. "What?" she shouted crossly. "What's so funny? I've done everything I can think of and I've gotten nowhere. No. Where. The last thing I need is you laughing at me!" She felt herself starting to cry out of sheer frustration.

"Hey! Janey! Don't." Jake's face softened. "I wasn't laughing at you. I was admiring your kick-assed-ness!" Jane laughed in spite of herself. "I love it when you give somebody a piece of your mind, Jane. You've got guts. C'm'ere." He waved her over to the couch.

"Guts, schmutz. What I don't have is results!" Jane wallowed, trying not to enjoy Jake's hands massaging her shoulders.

"You can't do this alone any more, Jane. You need … a … team … a team! Hey … why didn't I think … I just happen to have one of those!" He leapt up from the couch, bouncing the cats into the air and dumping Jane onto the floor. "Whoops … sorry! Gotta go! I've got an idea—tell you later, after practice." And with that, he snatched up his knapsack and tore out of the house.

Jane waited for a phone call that night, but none came. She checked her email. Nothing. Well, okay, she'd see him at school the next day. But she didn't. "I have no idea what he's up to or why he hasn't called," she wailed to Amy and Flory at the Shack after school that afternoon. "He just disappeared!"

"He's been busy," Amy said cryptically.

"Crusading god," Flory breathed, nodding.

"Shut up, Flor, or you'll ruin the surprise!" Amy whacked her on the arm.

"What? What surprise? You both know what's

going on and I don't?" Jane cried. But her friends wouldn't say a word.

That evening, after a dinner of casserole left-overs in the sole company of the cats, Jane sprawled on the couch flipping channels, seeing nothing. She was out of ideas as far as SeaKing was concerned, and the thought of arriving at the Center next week with that news made her feel physically ill. To top it off, her boyfriend had gone off the deep end and her best friends had jumped in after him. Not to mention her dad was still at the restaurant and her mom was still at work. As usual. *Nothing changes*, she thought. *Nothing ever changes, even if you want it to. Even if you try your hardest.* The images on the screen in front of her blurred.

The front doorbell rang, sending the cats scrambling down the stairs and Jane's heart racing. It was almost ten o'clock on a dark November night. Who would be wandering down the Rays' long, lonely drive at this hour? Except an axe murderer? She tiptoed down the stairs, and then shouted out in her best imitation man-voice, "Who's there?"

Jake's laugh pealed into the foyer from the other side of the door. "It's me, you big ogre!" he replied in a high-pitched squeak. "Let me in!"

Jane swung the door wide, grinning, and there was Jake, his smile even wider than hers, holding a half-foot-high stack of papers topped with a little black box. "Special delivery!"

She stood gaping at him until finally he said again, "Can I come in? It's freezing out here!"

They got settled upstairs in front of the fire, and Jake placed his bundles carefully on the coffee table in front of them. He seemed suddenly shy. Without looking at her, he said, "I took all the letters you wrote to SeaKing, Jane, copies of them, I mean, and I condensed them into one letter. Kind of a form letter to end all form letters," he laughed quietly. "I made a gazillion copies in my dad's office at home, and then I gave a stack to every guy on the basketball team at practice last night. We handed them out at school today, telling people what was going on and asking them to sign them." He looked up at her then, and slid the pile of papers across the table toward her. "They did."

Slowly, Jane reached out a hand to touch the stack of letters, but she kept her eyes on Jake's. For once in her life, she desperately wanted to have just the right words, to say exactly the right thing. "We'd better get these into the mail tomorrow," was what made it past the lump in her throat. Jake kissed her, as though he'd heard everything she didn't say.

"This one's for you, too," he said, handing her the small black box. Jane couldn't imagine what it might be. There was nothing else in the world she wanted right now. Lifting the lid, she caught a sparkle of silver. A thin chain, cut to catch the light, was nestled inside, and when she lifted it out, she saw the pendant hanging from it: a tiny, silver feather.

Jane was out of words, and Jake didn't need to hear any. He fastened the chain around her neck, and together they watched the fire until they heard the sound of Jane's mom's car pull into the garage.

18
TRIDENT

AMY AND FLORY PEERED OVER JANE'S SHOULDER and the three of them stared open-mouthed at the computer screen, rereading the email:

From: trident@tridentname.com
To: jane_ray@crseniorsecondary.com
Subject: SeaKing may have a secret
Dear Miss Ray,

I know you're trying to reveal the truth about what happened the day of the oil spill. You must talk to Jim Ellis. He was there. I wish I could do it myself, but I'm putting my job, and therefore my family, in great danger just by sending this email. I'll continue to help you any way I can, but please don't ask me to reveal my identity.
Sincerely,
Trident

They were at the Shack in the middle of a cold, dark November afternoon, the kind where the sun never quite manages to make an appearance, the kind where so few hours manage to squeeze themselves between the gray of morning and the black of night that it hardly seems worth it to get out of bed. Built into the ground on the northeast side of the MacGillivray house and connected to the basement via an underground passage, the Shack was small, cool in summer, and kept warm in winter by a sturdy little space heater. The friends had been using it as their private refuge ever since Malcolm MacGillivray had found the three little girls wedged between his gardening tools eating popsicles many long years ago. He'd moved his tools, Amy had hung a sign on the door and set her microscope up on the low wooden table, and that had been that.

At the moment, Amy was experimenting with corrosive agents on various types of metals in an attempt to create a retractable, rust-proof roofing mechanism for her brother's medicinal herb garden. Flory was tearing pages from fall fashion magazines and slotting them into a binder. She had categories for hair, shoes, pants and skirts, tops, dresses, jackets, and accessories, and used the binder each season to plan her wardrobe. Content not to be cleaning feces out of kennel cabs or fighting with algebra for once, Jane had decided to check her email and send a flirty little note to Jake. But when the Trident email appeared in her inbox, she forgot about everything else.

Trident again. She'd had one or two emails from that address before, but she'd trashed them assuming they were spam, or some marketing gimmick for the gum company. Agencies like her mom's sent out masses of that kind of crap to high school and university students all the time, under the guise of "cool." Jane knew kids who got ten or twenty every week. They just deleted them.

But here was Trident again, whoever he or she was. And with a subject line that couldn't be mistaken for spam. Trident knew who she was, and had figured out how to reach her. Maybe this was the crack in the SeaKing armor that she'd been looking for!

Amy broke in on her thoughts. "Some little chickenshit knows they should blow the whistle but they don't want to risk their precious six-figure salary," she snorted in disgust. "They probably saw Jane on TV just like everybody else and figured she could do their dirty work for them."

"She has a point, Jane. Maybe it's a trick!" Flory said. She seemed reluctant, though, to doubt the sincerity of the anonymous tip. "What do you think?"

"I think I want to talk to this person Trident mentions, this Jim Ellis," Jane said decisively.

"Uh, don't you think you should at least figure out who the heck 'this Jim Ellis' is before you go traipsing all over the city just because of some spam?" Amy was sounding more like her mom every day, Jane thought, but she didn't dare tell her so.

"Jane, let me try something," Flory said suddenly, motioning for Jane to give up her spot at the computer. She quickly navigated to Google's home page, typed "Jim Ellis Vancouver," and hit Search.

Nothing. Pages and pages of it.

"SEE?" Amy shouted triumphantly. "It's a hoax. Delete it, Jane, and let's go to Hilltop for hot cocoa."

"Wait," said Flory patiently. "I have another idea." She Googled SeaKing Shipping Pacific and clicked down through the first couple of pages to the company's contacts screen. She searched through the employee list—C, D, E ... Eckhert, Frank. Eden, George. Ellis, James. "Here he is!" she squealed, bouncing in the chair. "I knew it! I knew it!"

"Woohoo!" Jane crowed, shooting a triumphant glance at Amy. "Nice work, Detective Morales!" Flory beamed. "I do believe Mad Scientist MacGillivray will be buying the hot cocoa." Amy groaned.

"Flory," Jane was suddenly thoughtful. "Do that first Google search again, only use 'James' instead of 'Jim.'"

The first item that popped up on the screen linked to a press release put out by SeaKing the day after the canola spill. In addition to the story about an anchor puncturing the pipeline, which Jane had heard a million times by now, the release listed the names of the dock workers laid off after the spill. James Ellis was one of those names.

"So some guy with a gum fetish thinks Buddy Unemployment here'll blow the whistle to Jane," Amy summarized.

"I think the point," Jane said, "is that gum guy *knows there's a reason to blow the whistle*, which we've only been guessing up until now." She tapped the screen where Ellis's name appeared. "And he's saying he thinks this is the guy who knows the reason." She looked around at Amy and Flory. "I've got to talk to Jim Ellis."

Amy reached under the computer table and surfaced with a battered copy of the White Pages. Flory pulled her cell phone out of her purse and held it out to Jane. Jane's eyes went wide. "I'll make the call, but if he agrees to see me, you guys'll come too, won't you?"

"Of course, idiot," Flory said matter-of-factly, looking over at Amy for corroboration.

The little redhead grinned. She still wasn't sure she trusted Trident, but she knew there was no stopping Jane once she made up her mind. "Wouldn't miss it for the world."

19

CONFESSIONS

JANE DROVE, Amy navigated, and Flory recited the prayers of the holy rosary from the back seat. The directions Jim Ellis had provided to Jane over the phone led them to a small, run-down bungalow in North Vancouver, just east of Lonsdale and close enough to the railway tracks running behind the dock yards that Jane thought this Mr. Ellis must shake in his bed every time a train passed. Who'd buy a house in a place like this? Amy checked the number on her sheet of paper against the address painted on the sagging wooden gate. Yes, unfortunately, this was the place. She sighed, looking at Jane and then back at the house, as Flory cycled quickly through three Hail Marys and a Lord's Prayer.

Evenings in November were dark and crisp and scattered with stars, and before the Mazda's heater kicked in Jane had been able to see her breath in the air. She shivered. She'd told her mom she was going downtown with Amy and Flory to see a movie, and

Amy had told her parents the same thing. Neither of them had felt good about the lie, or about the fact that no one would know where they really were. Finally, Amy had called Mike on his cell and told him what they were doing, and said that if she hadn't checked in with him again by ten o'clock, to tell their parents. He'd done his best to talk her out of going at all, but in the end, she'd just said, "See ya!" and hung up the phone. Now, gazing up the walk at the dimly lit gray door, its paint chipped away around the dull brass knob, she almost wished she'd let him win this one.

Jane took a deep breath as Flory strung out the last of the prayers: "Despise not our petitions in our necessities but deliver us always from all dangers, O glorious and blessed …"

"Amen, already!" Jane blurted. "Okay. Let's go." She was out of the car and half way to the door before she could change her mind, and Amy and Flory scrambled to catch up with her.

Her polite taps elicited a thunderstorm of running feet and the sound of children's voices on the other side of the door. As the ruckus was brought under control by some unseen force, the door swung open and the girls found themselves facing an Ellis family portrait come to life: Mrs. Ellis, aproned and shod in slippers, straight, styleless brown hair and careworn hands making her look older than she probably was, her face that of a mother tigress—here, clearly, was the unseen force; three small boys and one very small girl, all of similar appearance and varying heights, each dressed in clothes more worn and colorless than the last, and gazing up at the visitors with identical wide blue eyes; and at the back of the little group, partly hidden by the hallway shadows, a tall, lanky figure dressed in faded denims, a white work shirt that had clearly been mended in several places, and an engineer's cap. Jim Ellis.

Jane realized with a shock that the family was as scared as she was. Her face relaxed into a wide smile and she held out her hand. "Hi, Mr. and Mrs. Ellis, I'm Jane Ray, and these are my friends Amy MacGillivray and Flory Morales." Mrs. Ellis's face softened slightly as she smiled back at the girls, and Jane realized she was pretty. The woman scooped the tiny girl into her arms and gently ushered the boys into the basement to play. She and her husband led them down the hallway toward a small room at the back of the house. Jane noted as they went that although the house displayed little in the way of luxury, it was clearly a home thanks to small touches like a vase of winter pansies here, hand-sewn curtains there.

"My husband thought you might like to sit in the family room so you could see his models," Mrs. Ellis said as they reached the end of the hall.

"Oh, great!" Amy muttered. "The guy's got nude centerfolds on his family room walls and we're supposed to enjoy this?" Flory glared and Jane stifled a nervous giggle.

Small and cozy, the Ellis family room was decorated like a ship's captain's bridge, complete with wooden captain's wheel, charts of Vancouver's coastal waters, and bookshelves filled with tomes on navigation, seaman's knots, and marine biology. Set atop the mantelpiece, the coffee table, and each of the book cases were the models Mrs. Ellis had spoken of—tall sailing ships and extravagant clipper ships, turn-of-the-century cruise liners and modern-day cargo vessels. There was even a model rail yard that looked remarkably like the one the girls had driven by on their way here.

Jane gasped. "They're beautiful!"

Jim Ellis turned and smiled shyly, and she saw his kind, worried face clearly for the first time. He, too, looked older than he was, and Jane could see that the recent layoff had taken its toll on this man whose life was already strained with care. She was suddenly eager to hear his story.

"Mr. Ellis," she started, "I know my phone call the other day must have seemed pretty weird, so I just wanted to say thanks again for letting us come and talk to you tonight." She blushed, not used to being the one to break the ice.

"Well, now, Jane, I hope you all will call me 'Jim' from now on, and yes indeed, it was something of a surprise to get your call." He paused and looked at his hands, seeming to collect his thoughts. "I must admit," he continued on slowly, "I was itching to tell somebody my side of things, but I got myself into a bit of a spot, you see, where I didn't know who I could trust ... other than my wife, of course." He looked embarrassed, and Jane nodded to encourage him to go on. "But then I realized you were the one who made that speech on the TV, about the animals, and how you weren't afraid to say it was SeaKing who caused the spill. And, well, I can't say I know what might come of it, but I thought you might just be the kind of person I could talk to." He looked slowly around at Amy and Flory, and then back at Jane. "I've got good instincts, Jane, always have had, and my instincts tell me I can trust you and your friends."

Jane glanced over at her friends in quick, silent communication, and then met Jim Ellis's gaze. "We feel the same way, Mr. ... uh, Jim." She frowned. "But there's something you should know. When I named SeaKing that day, I was only repeating something I'd heard. I've come to believe SeaKing is responsible for the spill, but so far nobody's found any evidence of that. I just can't prove it."

She looked up at him, hoping her revelation hadn't caused him to lose his confidence in her. On the contrary, his eyes were bright, and he was looking quickly from one girl to the other. His gaze met hers. "Well, now, Jane, I can tell you straight that you're absolutely right. It wasn't any accident that caused that spill. It was pure and simple negligence." He paused, and Jane held her breath. "And I've got the proof."

The three girls whooped and squealed and hugged one another, bouncing up and down on the Ellises' couch until Mrs. Ellis entered the room carrying a tray laden with glasses of warm milk and slices of buttered bread. "Sounds like it's going well so far," she smiled, and headed back to the kitchen.

Jane lifted her glass to make a toast, but Jim stopped her. "In the spirit of your confession, Jane, I've got one of my own to make," he said sheepishly. "I *had* the proof. I don't have it any more." Jane lowered her glass slowly, and the three girls stared at him in confusion. He sighed. "Well, now, maybe I'd better start at the beginning."

Slowly, Jim Ellis began to unwind the tale he'd kept secret for so long, like a ship dropping anchor, finally, in a safe harbor. Jane realized that she and her friends were hearing the first chapters of a story they'd entered somewhere in the middle. At last, things they'd only imagined or guessed at came to light, and pieces of the puzzle began to fit together in such a way that a startling picture began to emerge.

It had been Jim who'd first detected the canola spill, walking the loading berths on a routine check at about two o'clock that Sunday morning. Hearing an unusual sound, he'd shone his flashlight over the water in the direction of the American cargo ship they were loading, and was almost sick at the sight: a greenish yellow slick covered the surface and was spreading, fast. He cast his light in several directions, hoping to see the customary blue-black of the port waters at night, but everywhere he looked he saw oil.

He sounded the alarm immediately, which alerted the second engineer to shut off the flow of oil, and brought the other two night shift workers to the docks to begin emergency containment procedures. He called his Operations Manager, Wayde Coyne, at home, to notify him of the situation and to ask for emergency backup. There was no way his four-person night crew was going to be able to contain the spill with just one small boom and some absorbent pads. Wayde had argued with him, saying it would take too long and cost too much to round up a full crew at 2:00 a.m. on a Sunday, and to do his best with the resources he had. Over the next couple of hours, Jim kept expecting to see headlights and hear Wayde's ancient Oldsmobile pull into the lot, but the Operations Manager left his crew to manage the crisis on their own.

After hours of skimming oil, Jim could see by the pale light in the sky that he and his men were losing the battle. The amount of oil they'd managed to collect was negligible in comparison to what he could now see drifting across the Inlet toward the downtown harbor. Encouraging the three others to continue, in spite of the odds, he'd gone into the warehouse and placed an anonymous call to the local SPCA's twenty-four-hour line, letting them know there'd been a major canola spill and that the oil was headed toward Burrard Inlet's downtown shores. He assumed Wayde Coyne would alert the environmental authorities, but there was nothing in SeaKing company policy about saving animals. And after working the docks for twenty years, learning the names and calls of the scaups and mergansers, scoters and goldeneyes that migrated to these waters from the north each autumn, he could only imagine what devastation this spill would cause to them, as well as other birds and animals, before the great Pacific Ocean managed to break up the oil and return the Inlet's ecosystems to equilibrium.

Jane interrupted him. "But Jim, if your call was anonymous, I still don't understand how everybody at the UWRC knew it came from SeaKing."

"I think I do!" Flory jumped in. "You didn't think to block your call ... is that right, Jim? And so if the SPCA had call display, or hit last caller ID, they'd know right away where the call came from!"

"Well, now, Flory, I guess you must be right!" Jim looked at the girl in admiration. "I never did figure that part out. I just knew I was supposed to keep SeaKing's name out of things until it was clear what caused the spill." He paused. "Looking back on everything that's happened, I'm glad I didn't think to block that call."

He told them then how he and his men had stayed all day Sunday with the day crew, and then all Sunday night and Monday morning, skimming oil, cleaning the shoreline around the docks, and working with divers to secure and haul up the damaged pipeline. The line had looked diseased, with all its corroded sores and the one joint half severed like a broken bone, edges eaten away with rust. It hadn't looked nearly so bad on last inspection, but even then, Jim had fought Wayde's decision to continue using it until the end of the year. It wasn't worth the risk, he'd said in a letter to Alan Coyne. But in the end it seemed the CEO had decided it was.

When Alan had summoned Sunday's night crew to his office on Monday morning, Jim had assumed it was for a commendation for their extreme efforts and rapid emergency response. He'd hoped, too, for a mention of overtime pay in compensation for the thirty-six-hour shift they'd just put in. He had laughed, at first, when Alan told him he was laying him off. "The shareholders are insisting, Jim," Alan had said, his face gray and his hands trembling. "I'm sorry. If you'll just sign this, I'll make sure you and Margaret and the kids are taken care of for a few months until you can find yourself another job." He'd yelled then, drunk on fatigue and adrenaline and caffeine, and told his boss of twenty years where he could put his severance package. But in the end he'd signed it, thinking of Margaret and the boys at home, his baby girl, and wondering how he was going to find a new job at this point in his life.

He'd left Alan's office and gone straight to his men, telling them what to expect so they'd hear it from him first. And then he'd emptied his locker into a garbage bag and headed for his car.

Even now, he couldn't say what had made him turn back. He used the rear entrance to the warehouse, off the parking lot, and made his way quietly to the storage room. There was no one to see him, with all the staff either in the process of being laid off or out on the docks putting the new pipeline in place, and he was too exhausted to feel afraid. He didn't take the broken joint; it would have been missed right away. Instead, he chose a badly corroded one, the joint that likely would have been the next to leak. Wrapping it in plastic, he placed it carefully on top of his work boots and lunchbox and framed pictures of his children, hefted the sack over his shoulder, and went home.

"So there's proof!" Jane breathed, her voice tense with excitement. "SeaKing used a faulty line, so the spill is their responsibility. Now they'll *have* to pay for the cleanup, *and* the animal rescue!"

Jim closed his eyes briefly, shaking his head, and then looked back at Jane. "I took it back."

"WHAT?" Jane shouted, incredulous.

"Are you freakin' serious?" Amy wailed.

Flory was quiet, nodding. "You knew it was stealing, taking the piece of pipeline, and you didn't want to put your family at risk," she said softly, and saw the tears well up in the man's eyes.

He looked down at his hands and cleared his throat. "I wanted the truth to come out, but not at the expense of my wife and children. I wouldn't mind being called a thief if it was just myself I had to worry about, but they don't deserve a thief for a husband or a father."

"And so you took it back," Flory prompted.

"Yes. That night." He'd planned to leave it outside if necessary, but no one had changed the security code on the warehouse door or hired a new night crew, so he put the segment back in the storage room exactly where he'd found it. He was making his way back to the door up one of the side aisles when it had swung open suddenly and Wayde Coyne had walked in, dragging an enormous duffel bag behind him. Jim had wanted to bolt as soon as Wayde was safely ensconced in the storage room, but the noises he heard coming from the room had riveted him to the spot. He'd done enough pipeline repairs in his time to know exactly what was going on: Wayde was replacing the corroded joints with newer, intact ones. And, Jim had guessed, he would take the faulty joints away with him when he left.

He'd stood behind a shelving unit, waiting for Wayde to leave, when suddenly he'd lost his balance. Reaching out to steady himself, he'd knocked a glass container off the shelf and it had crashed like a cymbal on the concrete floor. In a split second, he weighed the risk of running against that of getting caught when Wayde turned on the lights, and chose the door.

"But you weren't the one tampering with evidence," Jane argued. "He was!"

"Jim wasn't an employee anymore, Jane," Flory said, still looking at Jim. "He was an illegal trespasser. He couldn't even risk being seen on the site."

"Right again," Jim nodded, looking impressed with Flory's reasoning. "Besides which, I can't fault a man for taking care of his family, now, can I?" He explained. "Alan Coyne is Wayde's uncle, and the only family that poor man has. I think in his mind, Wayde was just looking after his uncle. He owes that man his life—literally—and from what I saw, he'd go to just about any lengths to return that favor."

Jim pulled something from his back pocket. It was a photograph of the corroded segment he'd stolen and then returned. "I kept this, just so I'd always know the truth."

Jane held the photograph in her hand for a moment. "It looks..."

"Fake!" Amy finished. It did, like a torn up tin can with some red paint splashed on it. She let out a low whistle. "So we've got nothing." She looked around at the others in the room. "You show this to anybody, they're going to think it's a joke, just sour grapes from some pissed-off ex-employee trying to frame their boss. You tell the police about the 'real' pipeline, they find no evidence 'cuz Junior Coyne's gone and destroyed everything in the name of love, and meanwhile Jim here goes to jail for libel, theft, trespassing, and who the hell knows what else!"

Jim suddenly looked weary. "Well now, I guess this was just a waste of everybody's time, then."

He turned toward the doorway as the voices of his children drifted up from the basement. "I'll let you be on your way."

Flory pulled a business card from her purse and reached across the coffee table to give it to Jim. "You're on the right side of the law in one regard, Mr. Ellis. You were wrongfully dismissed. I can promise you one of my uncles would be happy to take the case, with nothing to pay unless you won a settlement." She smiled at him encouragingly. "Phone that number on Monday. I'll make sure they're expecting your call."

He rose and shook each of their hands. "I'll think about it," he said, and he turned and led them back down the hallway.

Jane stopped just short of the front door. "Mr. Ellis … Jim … we know the truth now. There has to be a way to tell it. Don't give up. We'll figure something out." He nodded and smiled, but didn't look hopeful. "The information you gave us tonight, we know it's confidential and it'll stay that way until we have a plan."

No one talked as Jane piloted the car back along Marine Drive and over the bridge. Each girl was mentally replaying the evening's startling conversation and trying to think of a way out of Jim's multi-layered predicament. Amy broke the silence with a primal holler. "What time is it?"

"Nine-fifty-eight!" Jane yelled back, matching her volume. "WHY?" Flory was laughing hysterically at the shouting match, just glad for the break in the tension.

"Because," Amy answered, still yelling but laughing now too, "if I don't call Mike RIGHT NOW, he and my parents are going to have a SWAT team at Jim Ellis's door in about two minutes!" She clutched her stomach, tears starting to roll. "Can you imagine what poor Jim Ellis would *think*?"

Flory lobbed her cell phone into the front seat, Amy made her call, and the three of them laughed all the way back to Cedar's Ridge.

20
TWO SHOTS

A LAN COYNE STARED THROUGH THE GLASS WALL
in his office at the back of his assistant's head.
The head was bobbing, probably in time to some of
that windy, watery relaxation music, as she sorted
the day's mail. She took longer to sort mail than any
other assistant he'd ever had. He knew it was because
she read the mail instead of just sorting it, but he
didn't mind. She often found little ways to soften the
blow of things like bills, client complaints, suppliers'
delays—with cappuccinos or baked goodies or interesting potted plants.

He smiled warmly up at her now as she entered
his office. Rachel Endersby had come to him following a difficult divorce, highly recommended by one
of his American colleagues, and the instant he'd met
the grandmotherly soul he'd known he wanted her
around the office. She wore her pale gold hair in a
substantial French roll, and eschewed traditional
business suits for Goddess Garb, long flowing things

in purples and turquoises that she ordered online. She was probably in her early fifties, not a grandmother at all, but what Alan liked was that she wasn't one of those twenty-something cutie patooties that was going to use the job as a stepping stone to somewhere else. Rachel Endersby would stay. He promoted her quickly from receptionist to personal assistant, and took it in stride when she refused to collect his dry cleaning or take his shoes for repairs. She brought him coffee twice a day, kept his fish tank clean, and forwarded inspirational sayings from some New Age listserve every morning, and he decided it was a fair trade. She was less business, more breath of fresh air, and lately he found himself relying on her presence just to get him through the day.

"You've got a letter from Jim Ellis," she said, placing it on his desk alongside a double cappuccino. The strong aroma both delighted and concerned him. Cappuccinos usually meant sketchy news.

"What does Mr. Power to the People want this time, eh? Eh, Rachel? Upgrades to the staff lunch-room? A new first aid kit? Afternoon nap times for all the dock workers?" Alan turned back to his paper-work, chuckling.

And then the laugh died in his throat and he looked up at Rachel, pen held aloft over the report he'd been about to sign. "Rachel," he asked, very slowly, "wasn't Ellis one of the ones we let go last month?" He lowered his hand. The man had no reason to be writing the CEO of SeaKing any more. Unless … "Is he … is he complaining about his settlement package?"

"No, sir," Rachel answered, clearly struggling to meet his gaze. "He says here he tried to refuse your settlement package." She cleared her throat and finished saying what had to be said. "Says he's suing you. For wrongful dismissal."

She turned to leave, and then suddenly seemed to remember something else. Alan could hardly tear his eyes from his own ghostly reflection in the glass wall. "Steel yourself, sir," she said quietly. "You've also got a, um, a package from the Ray girl."

She left him staring down at the two pieces of mail, one cool, elegant leaf of Morales & Monroy stationery and one six-inch stack of letters in a large manila envelope. Throughout the remainder of the morning, he never once shifted his gaze or stirred in his chair, and the cappuccino grew cold on his desk.

21
NOBODY GETS HURT

J AKE STOOD BEHIND JANE at the computer in his dad's study and ran his hands slowly through her long, dark, wet hair. A sudden rainstorm caught them on the way home from school, and they detoured to the Harbinsale house to shower and change.

Over the past couple of months, Jane had been thrilled to find Jake an eager confidant when it came to all the details of her campaign to get SeaKing to admit their responsibility for the oil spill. He'd also been ready to listen, and to hold her in his arms, each time she realized she'd failed again to get through. He kept her spirits up, saying he was sure they were reading her letters even if they weren't responding, and it was partly his support that had given her the confidence to keep fighting. After the overwhelming response to his campaign at school, and then the customary stoic silence from SeaKing after she'd mailed the stack of letters, it had been all she could do to refrain from repeating every word of Jim Ellis's revelations to him, and to enlist his help in figuring out a way to use the confidential information to force SeaKing's hand.

She knew she couldn't reveal the former SeaKing employee's secret without putting his whole family in terrible jeopardy. But she was desperate to bring the truth to light, and she'd run out of ideas. She'd decided, finally, that her last hope was to bluff.

"I'm changing my strategy, Jake!" she'd shouted to him as she combed out her hair in the upstairs bathroom. "So far, I've been operating on the assumption that we're all rational here, that the people at SeaKing think just like I do."

"Yep," from outside the door.

"Two months later, though, I've got nothing to show for that theory except a couple of form letters."

"Nope."

"So I'm going back to the beginning, to the original tip-off to the SPCA that mentioned a corroded pipeline. I've always believed that was accurate, that the lily-white investigation report was just some kind of cover-up. I don't have proof …" she took a deep breath, "… but SeaKing doesn't know that. I think I might just be able to convince them that I do!"

The door opened, and Jake stepped in, grinning, lifted her bodily and carried her down to the study saying, "Go for it! We just happen to have a computer available right now, and I'm sure my dad would love to contribute to the cause!"

Jane wasn't so sure of that herself, but said nothing to Jake. She reached now for his hands and placed them on her shoulders. "I can't concentrate when you do that! Let me finish, and then ..."

"And then what?" he asked, kissing the nape of her neck. She shivered and tossed her hair, which she realized belatedly probably didn't help matters as far as Jake was concerned.

"And then," she said breathily, "we'll walk to Hilltop and buy a stamp."

"Will you let me lick it for you?" he asked, completely undeterred.

"Jake Harbinsale!" she said in her best schoolteacher voice. "You *know* they're all self-adhesive these days!"

She'd won the volley, but he'd still win the game. Patiently, he drew up a chair and rested his chin on her shoulder, and watched as she addressed a letter to Alan Coyne.

November 29
Dear Sir,

This will be my final letter to SeaKing Shipping Pacific regarding the canola oil spill of October of this

year. Until now, I have trusted in your sense of respon-
sibility for the devastation the spill caused, whether or
not you were at fault, and in your intention to honor
your promise of a donation to the rescue organizations
that spent so much money and time trying to save the
wild animals caught in the spill.

You have given me no reason to continue to extend
such courtesies.

Please be advised that I have recently come into
possession of proof that your pipeline was not damaged
by outside forces, as your company claimed, but was
corroded and worn to the point that it leaked.

I am writing to provide you with the opportunity to
come forward with this information yourself, and I will
give you one week from today's date to do so. Should
you choose to ignore this opportunity and maintain
your innocence, I will ensure that this information is
directed to the proper authorities myself.

Thank you in advance for your cooperation.

Sincerely,
Jane Ray

"Holy crap, am I ever glad you don't talk like that
in real life," Jake said, admiration in his voice.

"Scary?" Jane asked.

"Very!"

He almost closed the letter on the screen before realizing it wasn't one of his own. He scanned it quickly and then read it through again before sitting heavily into his chair and reading it through a third time. *Stupid little* … she couldn't know. There was no way she could know. She was faking it, trying to get Al to panic. Which wouldn't take much these days.

He sat staring at the screen trying to decide what to do. There was no way he could risk letting this letter get to Alan Coyne. The CEO had gone off the proverbial deep end, repositioning wastepaper baskets and watering posies in his office like a broken man. It seemed like there was only one person around that damn place these days who knew what needed to be done and wasn't afraid to do it. He picked up his cell and hit a number on his speed dial. Be there … come on, be there.

"Hello?"

"Don't talk," he said quickly. "Just listen. I need you to intercept a letter. Yes, that's right. To Alan. From Jane Ray." He glanced at the date on the letter. "It should arrive tomorrow or the next day. Got it? Okay … no, hang on. There's something else … the little matter of the Ray girl herself."

He finished his conversation, confident things were in good hands, pocketed his phone, and emailed the documents he'd come for to the Club. When he got home tonight, he'd have to have a little man-to-man chat with that son of his about his choice in women. He'd put up with this Nancy Drew crap long enough, and using *his* study as her headquarters was the last straw. Enough games. Things were going to change, damn it, starting right now.

22
FLIGHT

J ANE ROSE SLOWLY to the surface of a deep sleep. Her torso and limbs were leaden, like concrete, and her eyes wouldn't open. She slid a heavy hand up to her face and rubbed her eyelids, brushing away the sleep and coaxing them open slightly. Through slits, she looked around her room, trying to orient herself. She felt as though she'd been away somewhere, and left part of her behind. She took in the gray morning light, Sweet Pea and Minnie nestled together on the pillow to the left of her head, the lulling rhythm of rain hitting leaves and roof and window panes, and the silence of the empty house. The time … 8:10.

She sucked in her breath and tried to sit up. But everything was too heavy, and she was far too tired. Even her brain felt muddled and thick. Wasn't it Thursday? Wasn't she supposed to be at the wildlife center? Why was it so hard to move? Maybe she was coming down with something. She reached up again to feel her forehead, and caught her hand on the thin chain around her neck. Her feather pendant. Jake. With a cry that woke her and sent the cats scrambling into the hallway, she tore at the little necklace, breaking the clasp, and threw it across the room.

The email had pinged into her mailbox last night, while she'd been instant-messaging with Amy on the computer in her mom's home office. `Time to Spread My Wings and Fly`, the subject line had read.

```
Jane,
    The past couple of months have been
great—thanks for everything. You're a
great person—never change. As we head
into a new year soon, it's time to try new
things and meet new people—experience
life to the utmost. I'm sure you will
want to do the same. Take care. Maybe
I'll see you in class some time.
From Jake

P.S. Please keep the feather to remember
me. I'll never forget you.
```

From Jake, not love. See you in class. I'll never forget you. Jane read the message three times before realizing she was holding her breath. She let it out in a rush and reached for the phone, punching in Jake's number. What *was* this? This was crazy. They'd spent the whole afternoon together just last week, and nothing had happened since. What was going on? These words didn't even sound like Jake, not the Jake she'd spent the autumn with. Not her Jake, who listened to her with that little smile on his lips and that light in his eyes, who told her every time he saw her how beautiful she was, who seemed to want to be touching her and holding her and kissing her as much as she wanted to be touching and holding and kissing him. God, don't think about that now. Don't cry, don't cry. This had to be a mistake.

"I'm sorry, Jane, he's not home at the moment. Could I take a message for you?" Mrs. Harbinsale was saying.

"Uh, no, no thank you. I'll … maybe I'll try his cell phone." *Call Failed: Not Available.*

She started to shake, a feeling of dread growing in her chest. This couldn't be happening. It didn't make any sense. It wasn't real. Turning back to the computer, she hit Reply, took a deep breath, and started to type. This had to be a mistake. She'd send him a light, quick, funny note, he'd explain, it would all go away. Love Jane. She clicked Send and counted to ten, trying to calm herself.

Ping!

Already? He must be online, too! But where? His mom had said he wasn't home. She gazed at the message in her mailbox. Message undeliverable. The destination user is not currently accepting mail from your address.

Jane went numb. Hugging her knees to her chest, she rocked back and forth in front of the computer, staring without blinking at the message on the screen. After several minutes, an instant message window popped up. Amy. "R U still there?"

As she typed out the words, she started to cry. "It's over with Jake. I don't know why." She shut down the computer, walked down the hall into her room, and lay face down on her bed. She was still crying when her mom got home from work, still crying when her dad tiptoed up the stairs that night, still crying when she finally fell asleep.

And now it *was* Thursday, and she *was* late for her shift at the Center, and she'd missed the signals and her morning run with Amy and Flory. Stumbling, still wearing yesterday's clothes, she made her way to the kitchen and called Evie to let her know she'd be there by 8:30. She snapped an elastic into her hair, grabbed a banana from the counter, and headed downstairs to find her boots. Only as she was backing her car up the driveway did she realize she'd forgotten to feed the cats.

Evie was drawing up medications in the exam room when she arrived at the Center. She glanced up distractedly and then focused again on filling syringes with the antibiotic fluid. "Jane, I'm going to need you to handle the care room on your own today. We're short a couple people, Avis is doing outsides by herself, and I need Katrina on meds with me."

"Oh. Sure. No problem." Jane shuffled past the reception desk and down the hall to the care room.

"Jane?" Evie had poked her head around the exam room door and was staring after her. "Are you okay?" She smiled. "I'm sorry if I sound a little grumpy." Her smile faded. "We had to lay Daniel off this week."

Jane walked back to where Evie was standing, not sure if she should give the senior staffer a hug. She also wasn't sure if she could receive a hug herself right now without starting to cry again. "Oil spill costs?" she asked, shoving her hands into her pockets.

Evie nodded. "That inspection report killed us. SeaKing came off looking squeaky clean, which I will never understand. And the donation they promised back in October never arrived. According to the law, no one was responsible for that spill." She sighed. "I don't suppose you've had a response from the bastards since the last time we talked?"

"I get it from my mom, I think," she laughed. "The business stuff, I mean. Well, maybe the scary stuff, too." The letter was a gamble. If SeaKing called her bluff, she had no more cards to play. She'd have to back down. She'd promised Jim Ellis that she would keep his secret safe.

She printed the letter and Jake folded it into an envelope from his dad's desk drawer. When she headed for the door, Jake grabbed her by the hand and spun her around to face him. "We are *not* going to waste precious time alone in this big empty house." He grinned at her, his dark eyes twinkling. "C'mon back upstairs. The stamp can wait."

Rand left his Caddy SUV running on the street and let himself in to his study. He hated coming home from the Golf Club in the middle of the day—Donna Lise or one of the kids always ended up wanting *something* and he invariably wound up stuck there for half an hour or more—but he'd done some work on the Christmas Gala at home last night and forgotten to email it to himself at the club, so there was no avoiding it. He listened: sweet blessed silence. Perfect. In, out, nobody gets hurt.

Jane shook her head and looked at the floor, willing herself not to spill Jim Ellis's story to Evie. Everything he'd said he'd told her in confidence, and she'd used the information to try to convince SeaKing to come forward with the truth. But they'd called her bluff, sitting tight, waiting to see what she would do. And she'd done nothing. There was nothing more she *could* do, not without giving Jim Ellis away. That would put his whole family in jeopardy. And that was a choice she just couldn't bring herself to make.

No, there was nothing more she could do. All her letters and all her emails had gone unanswered, probably tossed, unopened, into a waste paper basket beside some secretary's desk. Not one of her phone calls had made it past the receptionist. In fact, it was likely that nobody at SeaKing even knew she existed, even knew the name Jane Ray, let alone cared about what she had to say.

"I'm sorry," she managed to say, sure Evie wasn't aware of half of what she was sorry for. She retreated down the hallway and into the care room to make a list of the animals who needed diets. Six gulls, two song sparrows, one spotted towhee, a crow, five robins, four rock pigeons, one black-capped chickadee, two pine siskins, and a dark-eyed junco. Good grief. If she was going to get everybody fed on her own, she'd need a strategy. And the laundry would have to wait. She'd start with the small songbirds and work her way up to the crow and gulls. They were bigger; they could hold out a little longer.

In the kitchen, she put eggs on to boil, chopped apples, thawed plums, blueberries, and blackberries for the robins, and tried not to think about Jake. She refilled the wild bird seed bucket from the container in the storage shed, gathered leaves and small branches from the yard for the songbirds' caging, and tried not to replay the words of his email. She maneuvered around Avis, who was cutting fish for the outdoor gulls, and tried not to imagine the feeling of his hands in her hair, or the scent of his cologne on her clothes. When she bumped into Avis for the third time, the older woman grasped her by the shoulders and stared her down.

"What's gotten into you this morning, missy? You barely even said hello, and now you're bumbling around my kitchen like a blind bull in a china shop." She peered closely at Jane's face. "Boy troubles?"

Jane groaned. How did the woman always know? "You could say that," she managed to choke out.

"Well, now, I thought you and your young man were doing just fine!" Avis exclaimed. "What's happened?"

"So did I, Avis," Jane said quietly. "I don't *know* what happened. One day everything was great, and the next day I get an email saying 'See ya later!'"

Avis's eyes narrowed. "Are you telling me this Jake of yours broke it off using a computer?"

Jane nodded. "I tried to call him, but he wasn't home." A new thought occurred to her. "Or not taking my calls. So I tried to write him back, but his computer blocked my message. It's like ..." Jane felt her throat closing and her eyes welling up. "It's like he can say what he wants but I can't. He won't even let me talk to him."

Avis nodded, a frown creasing her forehead. "In my day, we had the 'Dear Jane' letter, too ... and the 'Dear John' letter, for that matter. Cowardice isn't limited to one sex or the other."

Cowardice? Jane was surprised. "Are you saying Jake's a coward?"

"I'm saying he didn't have the courage or the compassion to break it off with you face to face. He's afraid of something," Avis explained. "Now, from what you told me about him through the fall, I'd say it's not *you* he's afraid of. Quite the opposite, in fact. But he's afraid of something, mark my words."

"Well, so, maybe I could help him!" Jane exclaimed, feeling a tiny spring of hope. "Maybe I could change his mind."

Avis looked at her for a long time before speaking, the expression on her face mirroring the hurt Jane felt inside. "He's made his decision, my dear. And although he may have made it out of fear, he's also done everything he could to *prevent* you from changing his mind. I don't know why. There are a million different reasons why people don't finish what they start, relationships included. Not everyone has your courage, Jane."

Her courage. What courage? Jane made the rounds of the care room, gently wrapping birds in towels and placing them in a cardboard kennel as she cleaned their cages and replaced their diets with fresh food and water. Katrina worked silently, collecting in turn each bird that needed to be weighed and examined and receive medications. Jane tried to follow behind her and clean whenever a cage was empty, so that it was ready when Katrina returned with the bird.

Avis. What was Avis talking about? And what did she know, anyway? She'd been married for a hundred years, probably, and never had to worry about being dumped over the Internet by a guy who wouldn't even take her calls or answer her emails. She pushed the crow back into his kennel a little more roughly than she'd intended, and lifted the kennel cover to offer a soft apology.

The screen door banged and Avis bustled in from the outdoor pens, a large toweled bundle tucked under her arm. As she brushed past Jane, she said,

"It's Scotty. His breathing sounds strange and he's hardly touched his diet." She hurried on to the exam room to find Evie. Jane stood staring after her, heart racing. Not Scotty. Not after all this time.

Just as she was about to run to the exam room to see what was happening, Evie called for Katrina. "I've got a heron on the table in here, Kat. Can you come and get this scaup stabilized and start a respiratory exam? I have a feeling it's aspergillosis."

Fungal infection. Jane knew that much from her training manual. What she didn't know was how bad it was, or what chance Scotty had of pulling through it.

Fighting tears, she turned to one of the smallest cages, unclipped the covering sheet, and reached in to remove yesterday's food dishes. The song sparrow brushed past her hand like a breath and flew over her head.

She didn't have time to call "Bird out!" before she saw him land on the small ledge that formed between two large gulls' kennels sitting side by side against the back wall, and his head disappear through one of the air holes in the kennel. Dropping the food dishes to the floor with a clatter, she reached toward him as he flapped with all his might, his wings and body on the outside of the kennel and his head stuck on the inside. A few more seconds, and he would break his neck. If the gull inside didn't do it for him.

As gently as she could, Jane wrapped a hand around the flailing wings and stilled them against the tiny body. She felt the beating of the bird's heart like a trembling in her own hand. Slowly, she slid its head back through the hole. The head drooped, and the body went limp in her hand. "Evie!" she cried. "Evie!"

The head staffer was by her side in seconds. "It escaped and got its head caught in there," she said. She couldn't hold the tears back any longer. "I think it might have broken its neck." Evie gently gathered the little bird into her hands and examined its head and neck.

"It's not broken," she said, heading for ISO 1 and the incubator. "We'll get him on some heat and let him recover from the shock." Jane stood in the corner of the room, unable to move, until Evie returned. "Jane, we all do our best. It happens." Evie wrapped her in a hug and let her cry. "Just ask Avis. Hey, Avis, why don't you guys take your coffee break now? Super-Jane's done most of the insides and I'm sure Katrina wouldn't mind finishing up. This is perfect timing."

At the house, Jane sat at the table nibbling half-heartedly on one of Avis's peanut butter cookies as Avis refilled her coffee mug. "I killed a nestling once," Avis said brusquely. Jane stopped chewing and looked up at her. Avis nodded. "A baby chickadee. Barely out of the egg. I overfed it. It gaped and gaped, and I fed it and fed it. It didn't know when to stop, and neither did I. It's crop overfilled and it died, right there in front of me." She sat back down at the table and passed the cream to Jane.

"Everybody tried to comfort me and tell me it was an accident, that of course I hadn't *meant* to hurt it, that I'd never make the same mistake again." She shook her head. "But I could never bring myself to take the chance. I haven't fed nestlings since."

She finished her cookie and sat gazing out the window at the hummingbird garden, dormant now. "If you decide to let someone else handle the songbirds for a while, you know, until you get your confidence back, I, for one, won't question your decision."

Jane managed a slight smile, wondering how some people could hear you when you'd never said a word.

As they were walking back to the Care Center, a large truck pulled into the gravel lot, the logo of the local zoo emblazoned on the side. A woman of about twenty-five, dressed in a zoo uniform, hopped out of the cab. "Avis!" she called out, waving.

"Well, I'll be … it's Teresa! She used to work here many moons ago," Avis explained to Jane. They approached the truck, and Avis introduced Jane to the bubbly zoo worker.

"I was on my way to a school visit, realized I was way early, and decided to drop by! Come see who I've got with me!" She walked them round to the back of the truck and lifted the hatch. Jane gasped. Filling three quarters of the back of the truck was a cage, its sturdy bars made of reinforced steel. Inside it, chained to a steel ring fitted into the bed of the truck, was a cheetah.

"This is Freeman," Teresa said proudly. "Freeman, meet the girls!" At the sound of Teresa's voice, the cheetah started to purr. Jane listened, wide-eyed. He sounded just like Minnie. Only much louder. "Go ahead, you can pet him. He's really tame!"

Tentatively, Jane reached out her hand, and Freeman pressed his nose to the bars of the cage and sniffed. "How old is he?" Avis asked, looking as awed as Jane felt.

"He's been with the zoo about ten years, so I guess about twelve," Teresa replied. "He's probably only got a couple of years left. We've been trying to breed him—they're endangered, you know—but we haven't had any luck, and now he's blind. It's weird ... a lot of captive cheetahs go blind. There's nothing physiologically wrong with their eyes—they just stop seeing."

Jane stared into the large, round, blue-black eyes, unable to distinguish pupil from iris. This huge cat—almost four and a half feet long and weighing probably as much as she did, or more—was the fastest animal on earth. She'd read they could run up to seventy miles an hour. Which meant that Freeman could probably have crossed the length of his zoo enclosure in about two seconds. And now he was blind, and couldn't see to run at all. Or maybe he'd stopped seeing because there was nowhere to run.

As Jane gazed at the caged cheetah, on his way to some elementary school gymnasium to be petted and poked by a hundred milling children, she felt something inside of her, some tight little cocoon that had begun to unfurl during the fall, close up again. Like a door she'd almost walked through. Like Freeman's eyes.

They said goodbye to Freeman and Teresa and returned to the Care Center, where Jane discovered that Scotty was being moved back inside to be treated for aspergillosis, and that the tiny sparrow had died. She finished her morning rounds in silence. At home, she threw her clothes in the washing machine, pulled on her pajamas, closed the door to her room, and crawled back into bed.

23

JANE RAISES HER VOICE

"JANE?" Her mom tapped on the door. Jane held her breath, waiting for her to leave. "Jane, I'm coming in." Jane heard the handle turn and the door swing into the room.

"Go away!" she shouted from under the covers.

"No."

Jane tore the blanket back and stared at her mom, fury in her eyes. "Get *out*," she said, her voice low and deliberate. To her surprise and anger, Ellen ignored both her words and her tone, and remained unperturbed, seeming to study her, the way a scientist might if she were trying to determine an animal's character by its behavior.

"I'm worried about you, Jane," she said. "I know something happened with Jake, but two weeks of hiding out in this room is too much. When was the last time you washed those sheets?"

"You don't know *anything*," Jane spat back, and pulled the covers back over her head. Her mom had been leaving early in the morning and getting home late at night, focused on a launch campaign for a new magazine client. Jane was surprised she'd even noticed her daughter was home, let alone that she'd been spending more time than usual in her room. And how did she know about Jake? Had she been interrogating her friends?

"As a matter of fact, I know you've done nothing but go to school and then come home and go to bed for almost two weeks now. You've got friends who're wondering whether you're going to be able to run a half marathon with them, and people calling from the wildlife center asking if you're okay and if you're planning to come back to do your Thursday shift. I know plenty."

Jane felt a surge of guilt at the thought of Evie worrying about her. Since the last time they'd spoken, she'd become convinced that nothing she said or did made a speck of difference—certainly not for the animals at the Center—and that no one would notice whether she was there or not. Mr. See Ya Round Jake Harbinsale didn't care, that was for sure. SeaKing Shipping didn't know she was alive, let alone have any plans to respond to her pleas to help the animals. Hell, her own mother cared more about her precious corporate clients than she did about her. It had taken her two weeks to even notice anything was wrong, and even now, all she wanted her to do was snap out of it. Jane felt anger well up inside her, a surge of energy that felt good, powerful, strong in a way she hadn't felt for a very long time. Tearing the bedclothes back again, she turned on Ellen.

"You don't even know how to live your own life, so you can stop acting like you know anything about mine! Your marriage is a mess—did you, what, *forget* to get divorced? You and dad hardly ever see each other and when you do, all you do is fight about money—and I'm amazed you even noticed I was *here*, since you never are! Not once in two months did you invite Jake over for dinner … or Flory! Not once did you come down to the wildlife center to see what I was doing, or to meet Evie and Dan and Avis. Not once have you asked whether I'd heard back from SeaKing about money for the animals, which I *haven't*."

Jane was yelling through sobs now. "Maybe you just can't stand it that I'm trying to do something worthwhile when you spend all your time selling useless shit like fluff magazines and designer lip gloss to people who don't even need it. You think you're so good at marketing? Why don't you market dad's restaurant instead of always complaining how he never makes any money? It's good, you know, or you *would* know if you ever went. But that's just it … you don't. Nobody does. Nobody even knows it's there!" Jane smeared a hand across her eyes and nose. "It seems like you'd rather watch him fail than help him. And it's obvious you'd rather help your clients make their next million than help me with some dumb old oil company."

Jane stopped, spent, and took in her mom's face. She looked as though Jane had just run her down with her car. Badly hurt. Surprised. Terribly sad. Jane felt sick. She'd never meant it all to come out like that.

Ellen spoke quietly, not quite looking at Jane. "There's a roof over your head and food in the fridge right now because of the work I do." She cleared her throat. "I had to give up my charitable clients and my activist work because fluffy magazines and designer lip gloss pay more, and god knows we need the money. As for your father, I had no idea he wanted help. He never asked. And ... you're right, I never offered." Wearily, she raised a hand to her eyes. "As for my marriage—to the extent that it's any of your business—I'm the first one to admit I'm still learning. We both are. You're just starting to learn about relationships, Jane, and if you're lucky, and wise, you'll keep your heart open—in spite of whatever happened with Jake, and in spite of all the mistakes your foolish parents make—and meet wonderful people to keep on learning with all your life."

She looked at Jane now, and Jane saw that she was crying, too. "That's all I'm doing, Jane. I'm just learning. How to be your dad's partner. How to be *your* mother. I just wish you'd let me learn, or even *help* me learn, instead of insisting I get it perfect first time every time. Because I can tell you right now, I'm never going to get it perfect. Not by your standards or anybody else's. Life's just not like that. And it's never going to be like it was, either, if that's what you're hoping for. Things change. People change. But it's actually pretty good right now, if you'd care to notice."

Sweet Pea had come and lain down in a circle at Ellen's feet, and Minnie had made her way under the covers with Jane. When the front doorbell rang, both cats leapt up and ran out of the room. Ellen left to answer the door, closing Jane's door behind her.

Jane lay back on the pillows, running and rerunning her mom's words—and her own—in her head. It was as if four years' worth of conversations had gotten backed up behind a shut-off valve and somebody had just flipped the switch. For her mom, too, Jane realized. She wasn't the only one who'd been holding things in. It made her wonder what on earth her *dad* might have to say, given the chance.

She heard voices in the kitchen—who rang the doorbell on a Thursday afternoon, the Avon Lady?—and then the aroma of fresh brewed coffee wafted into the room. A minute later, there was a tap at her door. "Meals on Wheels!" a cheery voice called.

Avis? What the heck was Avis doing at her house?

"Um, come in!" Jane scrambled to make herself presentable but quickly gave up. There was no hiding the fact that she was in bed in sweats on a weekday afternoon. Avis walked in carrying a tray filled with coffee mugs, a cream jug, and a plate of homemade cookies, and made her way to Jane's bedside, taking the mounds of clothes, stacks of papers, and scattered books in stride.

"Mohammed doesn't come for coffee, we bring the coffee to Mohammed," she stated, handing Jane one of the steaming mugs and the jug of cream. She made herself comfortable on a chair heaped with laundry and sipped her coffee for a minute, as though this were all perfectly normal. "I lost someone too," she said suddenly, without preamble. "The grief takes your breath away."

Jane looked up at her elderly friend in surprise. Grief... Yes, that was it, Jane thought. No one had ever warned her about *grief*. She was only sixteen years old. But now there were animals, now there was Jake... Even her parents—her grief over the loss of the way they used to be with one another, the way they *all* used to be together. That was her grief, too.

"My first husband, Ralph, died of cancer," Avis said simply. "Ten years ago. Smoker. And for four years before that, the only way he could speak was to cover the tracheotomy tube hole in his throat. No voice, just a raspy whisper. You don't realize how fond you've become of the particular sound of a person's voice until it's gone." She blinked hard and then smiled at Jane. "Your voice will have that effect on someone special, Jane. Just you wait."

Jane shook her head. "I'm through with men."

Avis threw her head back and cackled. "Fat chance, missy! You'll be just like me, suitors clamoring for your hand." Her eyes twinkled naughtily. "After Ralph, I narrowed them down to two. One brought me roses, and the other gave me a backpack. Well, adventure beats romance any day, in my books, so I chose the backpack!"

"George?" Jane ventured a smile.

"George."

Jane thought over all she knew of her parents' courtship, at campus rallies, in smoky European cafés, in the mountains of Nepal. Her mom had chosen adventure, too, once upon a time.

"So," Avis abruptly changed her tack, "giving up the animal rescue business, are you?" Jane took a deep breath and almost laughed. There was no hiding from Avis. In a way, it was a relief to spend time with someone who wasn't afraid to say—or ask—*anything*.

"It hurts too much, Avis," she answered plainly.

"It hurts to see them suffer, and it hurts to know that we *make* them suffer so much of the time … humans, I mean. And you start to care about them so much that when they die…" She stopped, her throat tight, and shook her head. "It hurts too much."

Avis put a veined, arthritic hand over hers and nodded. "Better, perhaps, to leave their fate to people who don't care as much as you do."

Jane snapped her head up and found Avis staring at her intently. In a rush, she understood. It was always going to hurt. She loved them beyond any words she had for it, and because she did, she would try to help them. And some would suffer anyway, and some would die. And it would hurt. The alternatives—not to love them, or to leave their welfare to those who didn't love them—weren't choices at all.

They sat in silence for a few minutes, both of them thinking of animals they loved. As if on cue, Sweet Pea and Minnie wandered into the room, and Minnie hopped into Avis's lap and began to purr.

"Avis, what if you try to speak out and do something important for animals and nobody hears you?"

"Are you talking about SeaKing?" Jane nodded. "Well, first off, there's a big difference between not hearing and not responding. If you've been mailing your letters to the right address, they're hearing you, all right. They're just not responding."

"But why not?"

"They're scared, likely."

"Oh, Avis," Jane groaned. "You say that about everybody."

"Everybody who's got something to lose is scared, Jane. Why do you think it's so hard to tell the truth in this world? People invest a great deal—sometimes whole lifetimes—into maintaining certain lies. 'My father's not an alcoholic.' 'Cigarettes are completely safe.' 'We keep our oil lines in perfect working order one hundred percent of the time.' If you weren't so close to the truth, you'd probably have heard from them by now. Mark my words—you've got them scared."

"So how do I get them to respond?"

"Well, now, maybe you just need to turn up the volume a bit, raise your voice so a few other people overhear…"

The doorbell rang again, and the two-cat welcome committee left to greet the latest arrivals. Some hideout this is, Jane thought. But she was glad. Her thoughts over the past two weeks had driven her in circles and she'd been unable to get back on track on her own. She needed help, it turned out, and help, it seemed, had arrived.

This time in the forms of Amy MacGillivray and Florencia Morales. "Good lord, Jane Ray, sweats on a weekday? What's the world coming to? Hey … cookies! Mmm! Can I … oh, thanks!" Amy was a one-woman tornado.

Flory held out her hand. "Hi, you must be Avis! Jane has told us many wonderful things about you. I'm Flory and this is Amy."

Avis smiled warmly. "I'd have known you two anywhere!"

The girls joined Jane on the bed and together started pulling large, colorful plastic bags out of their knapsacks. "We've just been downtown to pick up our race packages for the Holiday Half," Flory breathed, handing one to Jane, "and you won't *believe* who's a sponsor!"

"Are you serious?" Jane was incredulous. She flipped frantically through the race booklet, searching for the sponsor page.

"Yep!" Amy couldn't wait through Flory's dramatic presentation of the news. "SeaKing Shipping!"

"We're going to boycott!" Flory announced triumphantly. "That'll show them!"

"What, not show up? Not race?" Jane asked, looking from Flory to Amy, and thinking of the hours of training they'd all put in.

"Radical, I know," Amy replied, "but on the upside, we'll get to sleep in on a Sunday for the first time in nine months. Uh … is that some facial expression I'm not familiar with, Jane? 'Cuz there's no way we can possibly support those guys, knowing … what we know."

Jane was staring at Avis and Avis was gazing back at her, a challenge in her eyes. Raise your voice, she'd said. So other people would overhear.

"Or…" Jane looked intently back at her two best friends, "we could tell fifteen thousand people what we know, in a single move."

For once, Amy was speechless. Flory and Avis stared at Jane, waiting for an explanation. "Amy," Jane began, "how well do you remember what that photograph looked like? The one of the corroded pipeline joint?" Avis's eyes widened.

"Pretty well, I guess," Amy answered, "but I'm sure I could ask for another look at it if I needed to. Why?"

Jane waved her question away. "Flory, do you think your uncles would let us into the Morales & Monroy offices the morning of the race?" Jane spoke quickly, warming to her idea. "We're going to need a head-quarters that's close to the start line. Oh, and maybe some walkie-talkies or cell phones?" Flory nodded, her mind racing to grasp what Jane was proposing.

"Could you use a little help from the media? You'd turn your audience of fifteen thousand into, oh, about a million, and the reporters will all be down there that day anyway." Ellen Ray stood just outside the bedroom doorway, her eyes on Jane, her expression a mixture of wariness and hope.

Jane looked up quickly, startled, and took it all in—the offer, the risk, the request. To help, to put her own professional reputation on the line, to be part of what Jane was trying to do. Slowly, Jane started to nod, and a hesitant smile lit her face. Avis beamed, and Amy and Flory began to whoop and holler as they all caught their first glimpse of what might be possible. Far from refusing to show up in protest of SeaKing's actions, they were going to turn race day into a show*down*.

"Wooooo, baby! Bring back the cameras… Jane Ray is ready for her close-up!" Amy shouted, bouncing on the bed.

"The question is," Jane laughed, "are *you* ready for *yours*? I'm not doing this alone!"

"Oh, so finally she decides to share a little of the limelight with her plebian friends," Amy joked to Flory. Flory ignored her and pulled a fresh black file folder and some blank paper from her bag.

"Let's tell the whole city what SeaKing did," she said fervently, pen poised. "Jane?"

Ellen joined the little contingent on the bed as Jane laid out her ideas. Seventeen cookies and two pots of coffee later, they had a plan.

24

AN OWL'S OMEN

IT WAS THE LAST THURSDAY BEFORE RACE DAY. The winding road into the woods, to the Center on the shore of Aerie Lake, was slick with black ice and edged with frost. The maples, birches, and beech trees were bare of leaves and empty of birds, but here and there in crooks and branches sat intricate bundles of twigs and moss, nests abandoned as the air had cooled and food had disappeared, but homes for the swallows, tanagers, and waxwings that would return in the spring. The old apple tree between the Care Center and the house reached knotted, gnarled arms to a gray sky as if asking to see one more new year. Winter was here.

Inside, Evie was drawing up meds in the exam room, ISO 1 was home to a single gray squirrel, ISO 2 was empty, and every last scrap of laundry sat folded neatly on the shelves. The cages in the care room were spread, one here, another there, around the perimeter, and the center of the room was bare. The large green and white aviaries stood empty and silent.

Jane found Avis in the kitchen mashing egg yolks. "There's nobody here!" she said. "Everybody's gone!"

"Gone!" Avis exclaimed. "Have you seen the outside board?"

Jane looked up at the map of the outside pens and started to laugh. Three herons, eight starlings, a western grebe, two each of sparrows, thrushes, and chickadees, a saw-whet owl someone had accidentally brought home in their Christmas tree, five squirrels, fifteen gulls, and thirty-six rock pigeons. "Welcome to winter at the UWRC!" Avis teased.

Jane had fretted about being rusty after the weeks away, and was nervous about working in the care room on her own. But the needs of the animal patients and the gentle rhythms of feeding and cleaning moved her surely around the room before her mind had a chance to wonder what to do next. The training and practice of the past two months had stuck. Humming to herself, Jane worked steadily, noting the differences between the grayish-brown fox sparrows with the little inverted Vs streaking their breasts, the song sparrows, rusty-brown and gray markings scattered over their crown, face, and breast, and the white-crowned sparrow, its black-and-white-striped head reminding her of a chicka-dee but its gray and brown and buff markings all sparrow. By 10:30, she was done. She helped Evie tube-feed a heron, and then returned to the kitchen to see if Avis wanted help.

"I'm just about to do the rock pigeons, and everybody else has been fed ... except the gulls," she said over her shoulder as she headed out the door laden with trays of seed, water and grit.

Fifteen gulls. Eight double diets. Setting out the dishes, Jane doled out cup after cup of large protein mix and then set to chopping a foot-long salmon into bite-sized chunks. Gazing out the kitchen window as she worked, her perspective shifted and she caught sight of her own reflection in the glass—long, dark hair pulled back in a low ponytail, long-sleeved yellow T-shirt, her UWRC name tag, and the silver glint of her feather pendant. Just yesterday, she'd retrieved it from the corner of her bedroom floor and repaired the delicate clasp as best she could, and then fastened it around her neck. If her mom had noticed it at dinner last night she hadn't said anything. Jane wasn't sure exactly why she'd decided to wear it again. It wasn't because she was pining—she wasn't, not any more. And it wasn't because she hoped he'd spot her wearing it at school. She'd heard rumors he had asked Leila Collins to the Snowflake Ball, but she hadn't seen him once since the beginning of December. She thought maybe she wore it to reassure herself that it had all really happened. His asking her out, calling her his hero, dancing with her at Cultus, and spending afternoons at Elfin, championing her campaign against SeaKing. The Jake she'd gone out with seemed to have appeared briefly in autumn and disappeared again with the approach of winter, like some rare, secretive bird. She knew that certain people—like Amy, for instance—brought aspects of Jane Ray to the surface that other people didn't. And that around others, like her mom, she felt she had to hide parts of herself—although that was starting to change, at least with her mom. Maybe she'd brought something out in Jake Harbinsale that he hadn't liked. Or that somebody else hadn't.

"Those pieces are too big, Jane," Avis said sharply, bustling in again with an armload of soiled towels. "Cut them smaller. Now, you're going to need to add some more liquid to that protein mix or it'll be too dry. Oh, and you've probably forgotten to sprinkle each diet with vitamin powder." She hurried away to the laundry room.

Jane shook her head, stung by the criticisms just when she thought she'd been doing so well her first day back. And then it occurred to her that Avis was just being Avis. Kind of how a crow was always a crow. At that thought, a giggle bubbled up to the surface. When Avis returned, Jane was leaning over the splayed salmon carcass, laughing as though she'd never stop. Avis took one look at her and started to laugh, too, and the two of them stood letting the wave of laughter roll over them and wiping their eyes for several minutes. Finally, Avis squeaked out, "What are we laughing about?" At which Jane bent double, clutching her sides.

"Oh, Avis," she gasped, "me! We're laughing at me!" She gazed into her friend's face, her lined cheeks bright from working outdoors and her ageless eyes lit with laughter. "Hey, don't you have some coffee to perk or something?"

Avis started, looking quickly up at the clock. "Gracious, is it eleven already? Time flies when you're making brunch for sixty-seven animals." Jane started to giggle again. "Meet me there in ten minutes precisely, missy!"

"Well, Jane?" Avis split the dregs between their two mugs. "Are you ready?"

"Hmmmph?" Jane mumbled through cookie. "For Sunday, you mean?" Avis nodded. Jane looked at her, her own face serious now. "I'm done with quitting, Avis. *Nothing* could stop me."

Avis nodded, smiling, and raised her mug. Jane

grinned and did the same. "Here's to having your say, Miss Ray!"

Jane clinked her mug against Avis's. "And here's to cranking the volume when I do!"

Just before noon, Jane was throwing a last load of laundry into the machines when she heard a blood-curdling scream from the parking lot. She froze. That sound wasn't human. It was the cry of an animal in terrible pain. She stepped out of the laundry room, almost colliding with Avis in the hallway, and together they rushed to reception, where Evie held the front door open for whoever was approaching. The scream came again, at close range this time, and Evie reached forward to take a large kennel out of the hands of the newcomer.

The fit young man, dressed neatly in a navy blue windbreaker and tan slacks, looked pale and shaken. He had obviously had to drive some distance with the suffering animal in his car. Avis stayed at the desk to take admissions information from him, and Jane followed Evie into the exam room keeping an ear tuned to the exchange in reception.

"It's some kind of owl, really big one," the man said in answer to Avis's inquiry. "I'm the pro on duty over at Cedar's Ridge Golf & Country Club. 'Bout half an hour ago one of our regular members came runnin' into the shop, says he hit his ball into the woods, saw somethin' fall from the tree, screamin' bloody murder." He paused as the owl let out another chilling screech from the exam room. "Like that. So I grabbed a couple towels an' jumped in the cart and headed over to where he said it fell, and there it was on the ground, flappin' and jumpin' around and makin' that noise. 'Zit gonna be okay?" The young man's voice wavered.

"No way of saying," Jane heard Avis respond. "We'll do whatever we can. Give us a call tomorrow if you like, and we'll tell you how it's doing."

Cedar's Ridge Golf & Country Club. Rand Harbinsale's club, Jane thought grimly. She wondered if Rand knew his golf pro had left his post to tend to an injured animal. She couldn't imagine Jake's father giving his blessing to an errand like that.

Lifting the towel gently away from the large body as Evie held its legs in gloved hands and supported its back, Jane steeled herself against the wrenching cries. It was a barred owl, almost eighteen inches high, her head swiveling rapidly as dark eyes searched the room for an escape.

Donning gloves, she took the owl from Evie, and the senior staffer gently ran skilled hands over the animal's body, searching for the site of the injury. Slowly, she extended one wing and then the other, and at this the raptor let out another ear-splitting screech. Gingerly, Evie moved her fingers down the leading edge of the left wing, stopping at the elbow. She pressed gently, her eyes focused inward, seeing in her mind's eye the bird's skeleton as it should be, and as it was.

"Shattered," she said quietly. "It's in pieces. Smashed by the ball." She looked up at Jane then. "We can't repair this. She'd never fly again, always be in pain." It seemed to Jane that she paused a moment before wrapping the towel gently around the keening bird, preparing it for euthanasia. "She'll never fly again," she repeated, as though to herself.

Jane saw again how the decisions made in this room were never black and white, never easy. By this time, Avis had said goodbye to the young golf pro and waited at the entrance to the exam room, watching. The three of them stood, immobile, until the animal's cries subsided.

Avis was the first to break the silence. "That Councilor Harbinsale has given us golf courses and new business centers and condo developments galore. All good things, if economics is all you care about. But I'll tell you, the non-human residents of Cedar's Ridge have not done well by Rand Harbinsale."

As Jane packed up her knapsack to leave, she said, "It feels like an omen—that owl."

"Nonsense!" Avis scoffed. "Don't even say such things." But Jane noticed as she said goodbye that Avis looked uneasy, too. She walked slowly to school, her anxious thoughts underscored by an owl's cries.

25
TRIDENT

FLORY SAT at the rickety wooden gardening table in the Shack, space heater aimed at her feet, ripping children's clothing ads out of parenting magazines. She was trying to decide whether to buy matching shirts and engineer's overalls, or four completely different outfits. When they'd gone back to the Ellises' to have another look at Jim's photograph of the corroded pipeline segment, the four Ellis children had greeted them at the door wearing exactly the same threadbare, colorless clothes the girls had seen them in over a month before. Flory had made up her mind then and there to forego a couple of wardrobe purchases for herself and send them a surprise package of brand new little outfits for Christmas. The overalls looked so cute, but they meant that little girl would be wearing hand-me-down overalls for the next five years. Flory shuddered. Unthinkable *faux pas*. Option Two it was.

Jane had swung by the Shack earlier to say hi and check her email before heading off to do a long run. She had two weeks of lost training time to make up for before the Holiday Half next Sunday. Amy had abandoned her corrosion experiments and disappeared through the trap door in search of hot drinks. How that girl could keep anything down around all these stinky chemicals was a mystery to Flory.

Ping! Flory glanced over at the computer. Jane must have forgotten to close her email inbox before she left.

Ping!

Ping!

The computer sounded like a slot machine hitting the jackpot. Flory counted fifteen pings before it fell silent, and curiosity overcame her reluctance to snoop in Jane's email. As she jiggled the mouse and the screen resolved, she felt her heart stop for a full second before it leapt into action again twice as fast as before. **YOU ARE IN DANGER!** the subject lines read. All fifteen of them, all the way down the screen. The messages were from Trident.

"AMY!" she screamed into the passageway below the trap door. "Amy! HELP! Jane's in trouble!" She heard a scuffling noise and muffled swearing a short distance down the passage, and them Amy's face emerged out of the darkness, whiter than Flory had seen it in a long time.

"Geez, Flory, I just dropped two perfectly good spiced apple ciders back there! This had better be good … Hey … what's wrong?" Flory's face didn't look so great either.

Flory pulled Amy over to the computer screen, and Amy hesitated only a second before sitting down and clicking open the first email message. Flory tried to stop her from reading it. "Are you nuts?" Amy cried. "This is serious, Flor. Jane won't be mad at us for wanting to protect her. And besides, she's the one who's always forgetting to log off. Lucky thing, in this case!"

All fifteen messages were the same:

Jane,

I am afraid you are in danger. I heard a conversation in which the words "take Jane Ray out of the running" were spoken. This is all I know. Do not take any unnecessary risks, and do not go out alone. I will try to find out more. Stay safe.

Trident

Leaping up and running to the door of the Shack, Amy stuck her head outside and yelled "JANE! JANE!" her voice easily loud enough to carry to the far side of Elfin Lake and beyond.

"Amy!? What the heck are you doing? Jane can't hear you!" Flory was staring incredulously at her bellowing friend.

"I'm sure she can, Flory. JANE! JANE! I've been told my voice travels quite far. JAAANE!"

"Unless you think it's traveling all the way to Stanley Park, you can stop your hollering and come up with another plan!" Flory cried, desperate.

"Huh?" Amy stopped short. "I thought you said she was out for a run!"

"She is! But not around the lake, you idiot. She's gone downtown to run the Stanley Park seawall!" Flory was nearly hysterical.

For one more precious second, the two girls stood staring at one another, panting from the effort of all their yelling. Then they turned and ran.

"What if we don't reach her in time?" Flory gasped, lagging behind Amy. "Why doesn't she carry a cell phone like normal people?"

"Why do my parents still drive a 1976 station wagon?" Amy puffed in reply. "Both fall into the same category of 'life's little mysteries.'" She grabbed a set of keys from inside the garage door and ran around to the driver's side of the shiny brown behemoth. "Let's just hope there's gas in the tank!"

"Let's just hope nobody sees me in this thing," Flory muttered under her breath.

"Suck it up, Batgirl, and get in!" Amy ordered, leaping into the driver's seat. "And if you happen to have those prayer beads with you, feel free to use them."

26
AMY TAKES A SWIM

JANE CHECKED HER WATCH: 29:10. She couldn't believe it. Two weeks away from her training and she was running faster, not slower. No heavy breathing or side cramps or sore shins, either. She flexed her arm muscles and clicked her heels and did a little dance from side to side. Who'd have thought taking time off could *help*? Never again would she ridicule anybody who claimed that rest was a valid strategy in a good training program.

She was alone on this part of the wall which, with forest on one side and ocean on the other, felt a lot like being alone in all the world. A float plane droned by overhead and she waved madly, like a castaway on a deserted island. In shadow for much of the day, the west leg of the wall was windy and cold. As she rounded a curve, she spotted the girders of the Lion's Gate Bridge up ahead, and looked forward to being out of the wind once she reached the far side.

She passed under the bridge at 34:27. Perfect. Still ahead of her usual time. She was suddenly aware of a presence behind her, running in step. Finally. It had been getting creepy with nobody around. She did a polite, under-the-arm peek. Black lycra running tights and well-worn trainers. Hm. Hard-core runner. And just a little uncomfortably close. She stepped up her pace, and the runner behind her stepped up his. She sped up again, and so did her shadow. She grinned.

She loved it when this happened. Once in a while on the lake trails, or on the track at school, another runner would come up alongside her, and instead of letting them pass, she'd increase her pace and match them stride for stride for a couple of laps, thanking them and waving them on their way when she was ready to return to her normal pace. It was a great way to build speed as well as experience the thrill of having your own free personal trainer. She'd done the same for other runners, and it created a kind of bond between strangers who understood exactly what it took to run a mile, or a marathon.

Breathing hard now, she decided to drop back to her earlier pace so that she could get an accurate gauge of her time around the park. She moved over to the edge of the wall to give the other runner room to pass, and started to turn her head to thank him for the company.

Strong hands gripped her shoulders and shoved, and she was over the wall before she had time to cry out. Later, she would remember thinking as she fell how lucky she was that the tide was high. The water rose up and hit her, as hard and cold as an iceberg. And then darkness. Eyes open, she watched shadowy, hulking, barnacled boulders and long strands of kelp and bubbles of her own breath rise up beside her as she sank, pulled seaward by an insistent current. There was no sound except the bubbles, just a peaceful, floating silence. Perfect, silent, peaceful. Her thinking wondering planning mind was ... blank.

And then her body took over. Lungs screamed for oxygen and limbs clawed through liquid ice as her eyes sought to focus on the small, wavering patch of light above her. Stay down, some voice in her head told her, even as she was fighting to reach the surface. Stay down. Don't give him another chance to finish you off. Her right arm struck a boulder and she wrapped her arms and legs around it, cutting her hands and knees on the barnacles that covered its surface. Half swimming, half climbing, she made her way to the surface, lungs burning, brain futilely trying to gain her bearings in relation to the seawall. Not a chance. Guess, damn it. Just pick a side. Breathe ... now!

The boulder rose about six inches above the water. Jane tilted her head back and pushed her nose and mouth above the surface line, sucking air in gasps she was sure could be heard all the way to the North Shore. She'd never realized before that air had flavor, and a scent. It was delicious. She had no idea whether she was hidden behind the rock or exposed to the seawall and visible to her attacker, so once she'd taken enough breaths to calm her heart, she pulled herself down below the surface and waited as long as she could before rising again to breathe.

After several cycles of breathing and then descending to wait, she realized she needed to think beyond this, to getting out of the water, getting warm again, and getting home. Home. She took another breath and descended again. Hugging the boulder with her legs, she brought her watch to her eyes and pressed the display light, thinking she would definitely be returning this thing if its water resistance failed her now. It worked. 40:23. That meant she'd been in the water for about six minutes. Or was it eight? Hypothermia set in after ten, she thought. She couldn't remember, but she was already cold, and was pretty sure she couldn't afford to find out.

She put an ear above the surface, thinking surely there must be other people on the seawall by now, and heard her own name. That was it, the first sign, hearing your own name. She was hypothermic already. She'd read somewhere that drowning was actually quite peaceful, and thought maybe if she just let go of the boulder ...

"Jane! JAAAAAANE!" Then again, she could be hearing the dulcet tones of Amy Airlie MacGillivray.

Heart bursting, she splashed to the surface, flailing her arms and calling, "Here! I'm over here!" Ragged and hoarse, her voice did nothing but sputter and squeak. She was crying. Not now, not now, she thought. Make some noise or they'll leave you behind. She tried again, but nothing came, and she was so very tired now. She kept waving her arms, but they were heavy and slow, and all she wanted to do was rest.

It was Flory who turned, scanning the Inlet. "Amy, look! A dolphin! That's good luck!" She pointed at a spot about thirty feet from shore.

"That's a rock, hallucinator. C'mon." Amy started running again. "Jane! JANE!"

"No, wait, *behind* the rock. It's ... what *is* that?"

Amy stood stock still, hands cupped around her eyes. Then she dropped to a crouch, yanked off her shoes and socks, and slipped over the edge of the seawall. She was at her friend's side in less than ten strokes, rolling her onto her back and supporting her under her arms to keep her head above the water as she sculled back to the wall. It took all of Amy's and Flory's strength to get Jane out of the water and onto solid ground; she was weak and cold and numb with shock. They wrung out her clothes, wrapped her bloody hands gently in Amy's socks, and rubbed her arms and legs, trying to generate some heat in her slender body. All the while, she stared, unblinking, out at the water.

"What's she looking at?" Flory whispered to Amy over Jane's head as she squeezed seawater out of her friend's long hair.

"Dunno," Amy answered, one eyebrow cocked. "Been in the water too long, I'd say." She looped her finger around her ear in the age-old sign for "crazy."

Jane's mouth curved upward in a small smile. "She saw the whole thing," she said quietly, motioning slightly with her head. Amy and Flory followed her gaze to the statue built on a massive rock that sat forty feet out from the seawall. Perched prettily on the rock, long hair streaming down her back and water lapping at her feet, the figure was a scuba diver, complete with mask and flippers, but most people thought of her as Vancouver's Mermaid. "She's the only one who did."

Jane blinked, finally, and looked up at her friends. "SeaKing did this, I know it. They're scared. They know we know the truth."

"*They're* scared?" Amy spluttered. "They've got nothing on me and Flory when we read that email from Trident!" They told her about getting the message that she was in danger, and the frantic drive down to the park.

"I was wondering how you guys knew to come after me," she said, adding with a wink, "and what *took* you so long!"

They helped her to her feet. "Now that you're talking, Miss Cryptic, I'd appreciate it if you'd tell us the whole story from the beginning, please. Say, my place? Over some homemade MacGillivray hot cocoa?" Amy suggested, shivering.

Jane shook her head. "I want to go home." Amy looked at Flory and then nodded at Jane.

"Flory, you drive Jane's car," Amy directed. "Jacques Cousteau here'll come with me."

Together, they cut back through the park, over the hill past Lumberman's Arch and the Aquarium and out toward the city. With Flory on her left and Amy on her right, her arms linked through theirs, Jane stumbled back to the car.

27

FLORY HOLDS COURT

E LLEN RAY BUSIED HERSELF putting the kettle on for tea and pulling oatmeal muffins out of the freezer to thaw in the microwave as she listened to the girls tell and retell the attack and rescue story. Jane and Amy had showered and changed into sweats, and were huddled now in front of the fire, each hugging a cat. Flory sat a short distance away on the couch, and the three fought to top one another in volume, exaggeration, and interpretive dramatizations of the various events in the saga. They could barely get the words out for laughing.

Ellen had yet to find any of it funny. Jane had been blue-lipped and shivering when she'd arrived home, but otherwise seemed unscathed in any way. Maybe all this silliness was therapeutic, she thought, but she wasn't convinced. Lips pressed together, she yanked the screaming kettle off the stove, filled the teapot and slammed the kettle back down on the burner. Turning, she pulled six steaming muffins from the microwave, and the kitchen filled with the aromas of ginger peach tea and the illusion of fresh baking. She laid food, plates, and napkins on a tray and headed for the living room.

"The best part," Amy gasped, looking up at Jane's mom through tears, "is how Flory thought Jane was a whale!" She collapsed again, barely able to breathe through her guffaws.

"The best part," Ellen replied, setting the tray roughly down on the coffee table, "is how Jane didn't die."

The room went quiet, except for the crackling of the fire. Amy and Flory looked at the floor. "Mom," Jane said finally, "I'm okay. My friends look after me. And you look after me," she added. "Nothing's going to happen."

"Don't forget Trident," Flory interjected. "If it wasn't for Trident, we wouldn't have known you were in trouble!" She explained to Jane's mom what they knew about their mysterious ally.

"Gum guy, eh?" Ellen asked, her curiosity momentarily overcoming her fear. "'Trident' sounds more like a code or a symbol to me."

Flory's eyes went wide in a physical expression of "eureka" they were all familiar with, and the three others watched as disparate pieces of information shifted and sorted and slotted together and reorganized themselves in her logical mind. When the calculations were complete, she blinked, and prepared to deliver her jewel of deductive reasoning like a bubble-gum machine offering up a perfect, round gumball.

"Trident," she announced, "is SeaKing!" The room went silent for the second time in five minutes.

Then Amy snorted. "I hate to break it to you, Flor, but you got your wires crossed this time. Think about it ... how can SeaKing be Jane's attacker *and* her ally? It doesn't make sense." She put on what she hoped was a sympathetic expression. "What ill-conceived theory led you to that erroneous conclusion, my friend?"

Flory shook her head, silky black hair swinging furiously about her face. "I'm right. I know it. Just listen." She laid out the pieces of the puzzle like a lawyer arguing a case. "First of all, Trident has had inside information about SeaKing all the way along. It was Trident who told us to track down Jim Ellis, and Jim turned out to have been the chief SeaKing employee on duty at the time of the spill. It's my theory that the clues he gave us about Wayde Coyne and the pipeline joints were things that even Trident didn't know about ... maybe still doesn't."

She took a sip of steaming tea, enjoying the fact that she now had an attentive audience, and continued. "Secondly, during our visit to the Ellis home, I noticed something that seemed important enough to store away in my memory, but not important enough to mention at the time. I didn't know what it meant." She paused for effect. "But now I do."

"In the name of the blindfolded queen of justice and the almighty Canadian Bar Association, Flory, would you *get on with it*?" Amy hollered. Ellen shushed her as Jane punched her on the shoulder.

"Carry on, Flory," Ellen prompted.

"Thank you, Mrs. Ray," Flory nodded, as if to the presiding judge. "As I was saying, I spotted a clue at the Ellis house, without realizing it. It was a letter from SeaKing, addressed to Mr. James Ellis. The envelope was a piece of the SeaKing corporate stationery, and featured a marine-blue embossed return address and logo in the upper left-hand corner. It was the logo that stuck in my head: a three-pronged pitchfork topped by a crown." She saw Jane's mom narrow her eyes and start to smile. "Ah, Mrs. Ray, I see you are following me down my little path of reasoning!"

"The final clue, buried deep in my memory but brought to the surface by Mrs. Ray's use of the word 'symbol,' is a lesson dating back to the classical studies course I took last year in third semester. We learned about the ancient Greek gods and goddesses, one of whom was the King of the Sea. He rules the winds and waves and all the creatures of the ocean, and the symbol of his power is the three-pronged scepter he holds in his hand. This scepter, good people of the jury, is called … a trident." She popped the last piece of her muffin into her mouth and grinned at her listeners, triumphant.

Amy let out a long, low whistle, amazed as always by the weird and wonderful way her friend's brain worked.

"So you see, Jane," Flory continued, "if I'm right, and you have to admit I usually am, *someone* at SeaKing is on your side. And is probably putting himself or herself in a lot of danger for the sake of helping you out."

"That's the problem, Flory," Ellen broke in. "There's way too much danger going around for my liking. This isn't just a polite letter-writing campaign any more. The attack on Jane has put the stakes through the roof." She paused, as if trying to make up her mind about something. "Jane, I think you need to consider backing out of this fight."

It took a moment for Jane to find her voice—but only a moment. "Mom!" Jane exclaimed. "Don't you see? That's exactly what they want me to do! They're scared! Just like Avis said. We must be getting close, or else they wouldn't be worried enough to attack me. If I back out now, they win. If we go ahead with our plans for the Holiday Half, well, who knows what could happen, but we have to try or we lose for sure. We can't give up now!"

Amy and Flory exchanged glances. This was a hundred-and-eighty-degree turn from the Jane of a couple weeks ago. They were afraid for their friend, too, but if she was prepared to keep fighting after everything that had happened, so were they. Amy leapt into the argument. "It's not like Jane's up against the whole corporation, necessarily, either, Mrs. Ray. You know? The attacker might be like Trident's opposite, just one bitter, twisted person with a lot to lose if SeaKing goes down. Am I right? Somebody help me out here."

Flory nodded, surprised. "She has a point, Mrs. Ray. The attacker may have been acting alone, without official backing from SeaKing, in which case we've got numbers on our side as well as justice."

"You girls argue a good case," Ellen conceded, "and I hate to be the voice of dissent here, but I still think it's too dangerous."

Jane bit the inside of her lip, frustrated, and felt herself shutting down. There was a part of her that still really wanted to quit, especially when she thought back to the feeling of those angry hands on her shoulders, and the terror of not being able to breathe. Her mom's words were potent fuel for her urge to leave the whole situation behind, to forget all about oil spills and dying birds and the struggling Ellis family and some psychopath who wanted her dead. But that was the problem—she couldn't. She couldn't unremember or unknow any of it. And she knew by now that she couldn't change the part of her that wanted to do something about it.

Suddenly, she leaned forward and pulled a ragged-edged scrapbook album out from under the coffee table. It was almost twenty years old, started before she was born by a young, idealistic, and very politically active Ellen Richmond. She flipped quickly through the pages, looking for the photos she wanted, as familiar with these images and stories as with the ones of her own childhood. "There!" she exclaimed, pointing. "My mom, the play-it-safe couch potato!"

On the left side of a page near the back of the book, one photograph showed her mother at twenty-five, dressed in a green T-shirt, cargo pants and combat boots, a scarf tied over her long, straight, dark hair and a Buddha pendant hanging from a cord around her neck. She was standing on the lawn in front of her parents' home in Vancouver, holding a hand-lettered sign that read STOP THE VIOLENCE, and smiling confidently at the photographer. Ellen's mother, Jane's grandmother, could just be seen in a window in the background, holding a small white bundle in her arms—Jane. The other photo, taken from the back seat of a car, framed the profile of her father's face and captured his hands on the wheel as well as the blurred face of another young man in the passenger seat as he was turning to speak. The young man held a cigarette, and the camera had caught the swirl of gray smoke that hung in the air between them. Both were smiling.

On the right-hand page, a faded news clipping headlined in large, bold type announced: LOCAL STUDENTS PROTEST TIANANMEN; MEET VIOLENCE. The photo, shot from above, probably from an office tower, showed a massive crowd of young students marching through a downtown street, the ones at the back of the march still oblivious to the fact that the ones at the front had just been tear-gassed by police. In this picture, no one was smiling.

Ellen's fingers played with a corner of the clipping that had come loose from the page. "It wasn't the same," she tried, knowing already that she'd lost. "I … we all went together. I wasn't alone."

Jane looked over at her best friends, and then back to her mom. "Neither am I. Heck, Flory just figured out that even my *enemy* is on my side!" She paused. "I have to try to convince SeaKing to take responsibility for what they did, mom. And I *will* do it alone if I have to."

Amy snorted. "Not likely, drama queen."

After a quick, awkward glance at Jane's mom, Flory said, "I'm with you, Jane."

All three girls looked at Ellen then. She gazed at Jane, the look in her daughter's eyes reflecting a determination she was intimately familiar with, but hadn't experienced in a very long time. "Oh, well, for goodness' sake, I haven't lost an argument this badly in a long time. Fine! I'm in. I'm in!" She shook her head, trying vainly not to smile. "Your dad'll kill me for letting you go ahead with the plan after what happened today."

"Let's face it, mom," Jane grinned, "it'll kill us both *not* to."

Ellen nodded, running her hand over the two photographs in the scrapbook, remembering.

"Now, where were we?" Amy broke in on her thoughts. She picked the teapot up from the hearth and reached across the coffee table. "May I pour you another cup of tea, Mrs. R? I don't believe you've heard the part yet where I pulled Jane out of the deadly undertow just in time to escape the shark attack."

28

GOOD NEWS, FOR ONCE

SATURDAY, THE DAY BEFORE THE RACE, Jane stopped by the wildlife center to remind Evie to watch Sunday's six o'clock news. There was no way to know whether their plan would work tomorrow. If they failed, the failure would be spectacular, and would likely still make headlines. But if they succeeded ... well, Jane hardly dared consider what that could mean for Evie and the animals at the UWRC.

"No way I'm waiting 'til six o'clock!" Evie exclaimed from the exam room as she bathed a gray squirrel suffering from mange. "I'll be in the stands tomorrow morning, girl, cheering you on! And so will Daniel and Avis and Anthony, by the way."

Her face grew serious, and she kept her focus on the little creature, gently swabbing the exposed skin. "I know we make a point of thanking our volunteers for all the time they put in here. We couldn't run this place without you guys. But I don't know if anybody's ever thanked you for what you've tried to do with

SeaKing—your letters and emails and the campaign at your school and everything. I have an idea how hard it was for you to put yourself on the line like that for the animals, and even though you've never gotten a response from the jerks, it really meant a lot—to all of us—that you tried. So … thanks."

Jane flushed, smiling, and looked at the floor. She hoped Evie would feel the same way after tomorrow.

"Which brings me to some *good* news, for once!" Evie continued. "A grant came through today, a big one. It means that we're going to be able to put a rescue team on the road next summer." Evie beamed. "Can you believe it?"

Jane let out a muffled whoop, mindful of the animals nearby. This was big news! It made her heart ache every time they had to tell a caller they couldn't pick up an injured animal because they didn't have a vehicle or enough staff. Now they'd be able to go wherever the animals needed them.

"We're getting one of those new environmentally friendly cars, and money to hire dedicated rescue staff for the whole summer. So …" Evie looked pointedly at Jane. "How would you like to be part of the team?"

"*Me*?" Jane was sure she'd misunderstood.

"Avis said I couldn't offer you a job unless I promised to let you work the Thursday morning shift on site. Something about a sacred coffee break, I think she said."

Jane stood rooted to the spot, shaking her head. She couldn't believe the opportunity Evie was offering her, a gift she'd never asked for, or even dreamed of. A year ago, she hadn't been able to tell a sparrow from a siskin, and now she was going to be part of the rescue and rehabilitation team here at the Center. A year ago, Amy was the mad scientist, Flory was the lawyer, and she was just plain Jane, still wondering what on this earth she wanted to be when she grew up. Now, she thought, she might just have a clue.

"Uh, Jane? You with me?" Evie wrapped the squirrel in a soft cloth and passed it to a volunteer to return to its cage. "I mean, it's a student wage, for sure, and the days'll be long, and there'll be some danger involved, but …"

"Yes!" Jane practically shouted. "Yes! I'm in! I want the job! It sounds like heaven!"

Evie laughed at that, and said she'd call as soon as they had a contract for Jane to sign. "That's the thing about everybody here," she mused. "We clean cages and dirty laundry and look at feces under microscopes and get vomited on and feed animals from morning 'til night, sun or snow. And we wouldn't trade it for anything in the world." She walked around the desk and gave Jane a hug. "You fit right in. See you tomorrow."

29
RACE DAY

At 5:59, jane reached over and turned off her alarm clock. She'd been awake for almost half an hour already, Minnie warm on her chest and Sweet Pea curled in the crook of her right arm. Her room was still dark; one of the longest days of the year, it would be over an hour yet before she saw daylight. The dark reminded her of an unopened gift, like the wrapping on a new day. Last night's sunset had come early, taking its cue from the gray mist that had shrouded the city for much of the day. There had been talk of snow, though nothing more than talk, but Jane could feel that the temperature had dropped again overnight.

She turned her head back to check the clock, and watched it relinquish night for morning. Six a.m. As if the clock were wired to her nervous system, she felt a sudden surge of adrenaline shoot through her core, wrap itself around her diaphragm and cut off her breath. Her mouth went dry and her heart thumped once, twice, before revving itself into a panicked rattle. An urgent cramp grabbed hold of her gut and squeezed, and she was out of bed and halfway to the bathroom. "Sorry, guys!" she apologized to the flying cats. "Nature calls!" She marveled again at the power of the flight or fight response to remind her that she was, first and last, an animal.

A duck, to be precise. She giggled, picturing the scene to come, and then almost threw up as the thought of the job that lay ahead blasted another hit of adrenaline into her bloodstream. Drawing in her thoughts, she took a couple of slow, deep breaths and deliberately calmed her mind. Her body followed. She was going to need to be able to keep some food down if she wanted to go the distance today.

It was race day. Thirteen grueling miles through downtown Vancouver, not to mention the showdown with SeaKing. All before most people in the city would even be out of bed. This was it, her last chance to prove that SeaKing was at fault for the canola oil spill earlier this year. She'd given them every opportunity to come forward with the truth on their own, and yet they'd hidden and lied and covered up and convinced the city it had all been an unfortunate accident. If the plan worked, everyone in Vancouver would know by dinnertime tonight that SeaKing Shipping was responsible for the spill. If something went wrong, however … well, for the sake of the tail end of her digestive system, she decided she couldn't afford to think about that right now.

There was a tap on the bathroom door. Her mom was up, too. She felt her breathing deepen a little further as she remembered she would have company this morning. She wasn't in this alone. "Hey, honey, can you hurry? It's getting kind of urgent out here." Jane started to laugh. She pictured Amy's and Flory's bathroom lights on, and then a scattered constellation of bathroom lights twinkling in the dark as marathoners and half-marathoners all over the city dealt with pre-race jitters in the way the body knew best.

When she opened the door, her mom was crouched on the floor outside, holding her stomach. "Um, you might want to wait a few minutes before you go in there," Jane warned her.

"Can't," her mom answered, before pitching forward and slamming the door behind her.

"You're not even racing today!" Jane called through the door, laughing. Back in her room, Sweet Pea and Minnie had hunkered back into the warm bed Jane had left behind. She bent down to kiss the top of each little head before slipping into her reflective running gear and pulling her hair back into a low ponytail. At exactly 6:15, she went to the window and ran through the signals with Amy and Flory. Good—they were both up … *and* out of the bathroom.

In the kitchen, she put the coffee on for her mom, set out a protein bar and a sports drink to take with her later, and made a toasted peanut butter and banana bagel. After downing a glass of orange juice, she grabbed her flashlight, a water bottle, and the bagel, and headed out to the trails. To walk, to move, to wake up. To warm up. To calm down.

Amy and Flory were waiting for her at the head of the trail, flashlights in hand and Buster in tow. Amy flicked a mittened hand in a small wave and Flory managed a half smile. They were both pale—scared, Jane realized. Together, they walked the long trail to the far side of Elfin Lake in silence, dead and dormant grasses, rushes, and salmonberry bushes rustling in an icy, dry breeze. As they circled back, Jane spotted the night lights on Grouse Mountain, strings of far-away Christmas lights rising up to the clouds and disappearing in the dark sky. "Make a wish," she whispered, pointing. They stood still, eyes closed, each making the same wish in her own way, until Buster tugged on his leash and drew them onward again.

At 7:20, they dropped Buster off at the MacGillivrays' and at 7:28 arrived, rosy-cheeked and sweating, back at the Rays' carport. Jane's mom was racing between the house and the car, stuffing knapsacks into the already crammed trunk of her Volvo.

The calm Jane had managed to find on the trails over the past hour started to evaporate. She glanced at the basement door and then looked at her mom. "Dad coming?" she asked, trying to sound like she didn't care.

"Oh, Jane," her mom began, and Jane knew the answer before she could say any more. "I almost forgot. He asked me to give you this." She reached into the pocket of her jacket. "You know the only day he has to sleep in a little is Sunday. Maybe we'll drop by the restaurant this afternoon and let him know how it went." She handed Jane a small, carefully folded piece of paper. Jane opened it slowly, wishing she could read it by herself, but knowing she wouldn't get a moment alone for the next several hours.

The words were printed in pencil, in an almost childlike hand. *See Jane run. Run, Jane, run*! He had drawn and colored a little stick figure in a red polka-dotted dress. She was smiling and waving as she ran across the page, legs spinning like a pinwheel and hair flying. *I love you. Dad. xoxo* She crouched down next to the car and retied both her shoes, then pulled a tissue from the pocket of her jacket and blew her nose. Refolding the note, she zipped it into the pocket. "Seven-thirty!" her mom called. "Time to go!"

They climbed into the car, Ellen at the wheel and Jane in the passenger seat, Amy and Flory in the back, and headed for the downtown core. They'd spent the past three weeks defining and rehearsing every detail of their plan and now, it seemed, there was nothing more to say. Even Amy was silent. More than anything else, this worried Jane. She counted on her friend's sense of humor and her ability to chatter on at length about the stupidest of subjects to get her through times like this.

She heard a low growl from the back seat. Good grief! Had they brought along one of the cats by accident? She turned to look, and the sound came again, a deep, gurgling rumble that ended in a high-pitched fizz. Amy's eyes were on the ceiling of the car, but when the sound started up again she clapped a hand to her stomach.

"Mrs. Ray, where did you pack those protein bars? I don't know about the rest of you people, but I just flushed last night's pasta dinner down the toilet. I'm *starving!*"

Flory snorted, Amy's stomach barked out another loud growl, and then the whole car erupted in laughter. The four of them giggled and chattered and gorged themselves on protein bars and water the rest of the way downtown.

30
HEADQUARTERS

THE RESEARCH LIBRARY AT MORALES & MONROY, Barristers and Solicitors, looked like the dressing rooms for a production of Alfred Hitchcock's *The Birds*. Black, brown, gray, and white feathers lay strewn on the carpet below the three, four-foot-high bird costumes that hung from one of the library ladders. They'd purchased the tattered old mascot uniforms from Cedar's Ridge Senior Secondary's athletics department, and Jane and Avis had renovated and reupholstered them with the entire stock of feathers from the local hobby shop. If you didn't look too closely, they resembled a male surf scoter—Jane had insisted on that one—a lesser scaup, and a glaucous-winged gull.

Flory checked her watch. "It's eight twenty-five, everybody. We're down to twenty minutes." She looked around to make sure all eyes were on her. "Let's get dressed, and Mrs. Ray, if you could run us through the communication procedure one more time." Ellen helped Jane into the scoter costume, and then zipped Flory into the scaup and Amy into the gull, all the while calling cues and checking their responses. Once each girl had her head piece on, she took a couple of steps back to assess the full effect. She'd been afraid they would simply look funny, laughable. But in fact the effect was startling, disturbing somehow, the way mimes and marionettes and giant clowns on stilts were nightmarish versions of children's toys. She shivered. They weren't even finished yet.

"Okay," Flory's muffled voice emanated from somewhere below the scaup's bill, "the cell phones are in that bag on the table, Mrs. Ray. They're labeled." Ellen withdrew the three little phones, one labeled MOTHERSHIP 2 MEDIA, the second labeled MOTHERSHIP 2 RACERS, and the third, RACERS 2 MOTHERSHIP. She handed this last one to Flory along with a headset, clipped the second to her belt loop, and flipped open the first to check the pre-set text message and the group-send list one final time.

"Eight-thirty-five," Flory called. "Mothership to the stands."

"Bye, mom," Jane called. "Good luck!" She flapped a wing, and Ellen laughed.

"See you down there, girls," she called back, slipping on her headset as the elevator door closed.

"Unlikely you'll *avoid* seeing us," Amy muttered.

"What was that, Racer Three?" Flory barked.

"Racer Three my ass, Flory Morales!" Amy retorted.

"Hey, hey, hey," Jane broke in. "Quit your fighting for one minute and come check out this scene." She was standing at the window facing the Plaza of Nations just two blocks away. Morales & Monroy had the seventh floor of the tower and, at the moment, a bird's eye view of the starting line for the Vancouver International Holiday Marathon. Clogged with runners stretching, stowing gear, and lining up for the porta-potties, the boulevard had been transformed from a city street into a winter carnival. Music blared from massive, pole-top speakers, and two impossibly perky dancers had taken the stage to lead a group of marathoners through an aerobic warm-up routine. The stands were filled with warmly bundled spectators and well-wishers, and Jane wondered if anybody was still in bed this Sunday morning.

A digital clock mounted above the stage counted down to the start of the half-marathon at 9:00 a.m. The full marathon would start at 9:15. It was now 8:39. She felt a familiar surge and wondered if it were possible for a body to run dry of adrenaline.

8:40. Flory's cell phone rang. She let her left wing hang lamely and pulled her arm inside her costume.

"Racers in headquarters," she answered, and then listened for a moment. "Roger that. Over." She started for the elevator. "That was your mom, Jane. She's in position in the stands and has the sponsors in sight—all of them accounted for." She paused. "This is it!"

Jane shook her head. This was crazy. She couldn't do this in front of all those people. What if Jim Ellis had been wrong? What if … Amy kicked her in the tail feathers and shoved her up roughly in front of the elevator. "Take a good look at yourself, Chicken Little, and remember who you're doing this for." Jane gazed at the big, black, blurry image in the steel doors. Sylvester—her scoter. Or herself. She wasn't sure which Amy had meant, but it didn't matter. She was right either way. The elevator door slid noiselessly open, and three large water birds stepped inside.

31
FIGHT

"**H**OLD STILL AND HOLD YOUR BREATH," Amy commanded. Jane gulped in air and plugged her nose, and Amy lofted the can of spray-on cooking oil. They were standing in the Folio Tower lobby, elegantly appointed in luminous arched marble, brocade-upholstered antique furniture and a plush scarlet carpet, looking more than a little out of place. They had three minutes before Jane's mom would expect to see them approach the start line. "Wow … I can hardly make myself do this."

"We're at 8:42, Racer Three … er, Amy," Flory said, an unusual edge in her voice. "There's no Plan B. If you can't do it, I will."

"Do it, Ame," Jane whispered through her mask. "Make it look awful. It *was* awful."

Amy covered Jane's costume with a thorough coating of oil, not so much that it dripped, but enough so that she glistened unmistakably from crown feathers to tail. Jane felt the weight it added, and thought about the birds she'd held and cared for that fall, their hollow bones, their mysterious marriage of lightness and strength. If she let herself, she could feel trapped inside this cumbersome, ruined suit. But she wasn't. Whenever she wanted, she could unzip it and step out.

She watched Amy spray Flory's scaup, and Flory coat Amy's gull. The sight made her sick, and sad. And angry. Oh, glory! There it was. The fight part. For the past three and a half hours, she'd been ready to crawl back under the covers, lock herself in the bathroom, get lost in the lake trails, take the wrong exit off the highway, hit the panic button in the elevator and stay stuck between floors for the duration of the marathon. But there it was. There it was.

Flory's cell phone rang. "Racers in Folio Tower lobby," she answered, and then listened. "We copy. We're ready. Over." She slapped the phone shut and turned to Amy and Jane. "They're getting ready to announce the race sponsors," she said. "It's now or never."

Amy would say later that it sounded like the cry of the clansmen on the battlefields of ancient Scotland. Jane shouted "Now!" and it rang off the pillars and reverberated across the archways and spurred Amy and Flory to add their voices: "Now!" And a hundred echoed voices joined theirs and they shouted one more time before racing through the door: "NOOOOOOW!"

"... and just to my right, ladies and gentlemen, we have the makers of Pro-Bar Protein Energy Bars, Holiday Marathon sponsors for five years *running* (heh heh) and providers of the energizing snacks you runners will be able to chase down with Sandollar Springs natural spring water at ten refreshment stations along the marathon route. I'm Rock Hamilton, with CKTS-Vancouver radio, broadcasting live today from the start *and* finish line of the nineteenth annual Vancouver International Holiday Marathon." From half a block away, Jane recognized the deep, resonant voice from the radio station her mom listened to in the car. He was a friend of her mom's, someone she'd dated before she'd met Jane's dad, and Ellen had included him in this morning's plans. He didn't know exactly what to expect, only to expect *something*, to be prepared to commentate and, if necessary, direct events if things got a little out of hand.

"I'd like to introduce to you our final sponsor, new to the Holiday Marathon family this year. Ladies and gentlemen, please welcome SeaKing

Shipping Pacific." They were close enough now that Jane could make out individual faces in the stands. There were the four SeaKing executives: CEO Alan Coyne, Operations Manager and the CEO's nephew Wayde Coyne, Chief Financial Officer Mason Choi, and Public Relations Director Belinda Lee. Flory had researched Internet records, newspaper clippings, and even old high-school yearbooks to find pictures of the four, so that they'd recognize them on race day. Suddenly Jane stopped walking—there were two more familiar faces in the stand, faces she hadn't expected to see today, or perhaps ever again: Jake Harbinsale and his dad, Rand. What were they doing here? And what were they doing in the sponsor stand? Jane wondered briefly if Jake had come to see her run, but dismissed the thought sadly. That wasn't possible, not after the email he'd sent.

Amy and Flory had turned around, realizing she was trailing behind. "Jake's here," she said. Both her friends nodded.

"We saw him earlier," Flory replied. "We just hoped you hadn't."

"… ships canola oil all over the world," Rock Hamilton was saying. "It's a pure, home-grown Canadian harvest—canola means 'Canadian oil.' And SeaKing's the reason it's on your cooking shelf, on your salads, on your … b-birds?

"Ladies and gentlemen, CKTS listeners, three gigantic birds have just stepped onto the boulevard and are making their way toward the start line! I don't know what to make of this, and neither does the crowd! We've got one black, one brown, one gray ... uh, with a knapsack, that gray one, and I'm no ornithologist, but they look like two ducks and a seagull to me! A seagull with a knapsack! Heh heh! SeaKing CEO Alan Coyne, you're a sailing man. Do these creatures look familiar to *you*? Er, Mr. Coyne?

"Well! We have got a *situation* on our hands down here at the Plaza of Nations, ladies and gentlemen! It's just twelve short minutes before the start of the Vancouver International Holiday Marathon, three exceedingly large birds have entered the fray here at the starting line, and our new sponsors from SeaKing Shipping have just left the stands and are headed toward the birds! *What* is going *on*? Are they mascots? YES! Ladies and gentlemen, these six-foot-tall birds have just unveiled signs that say SeaKing! What a nice surprise from our new sponsors—a little pre-race entertainment here at Plaza of Nations, where...

"Oh! Pardon *me*! Those birds are covered in oil! I stand corrected, ladies and gentlemen, this is *not* a happy little mascot moment for SeaKing Shipping. Those signs the birds are carrying ... a few feet closer and I'll be able to tell you what those signs say about SeaKing. Is this someone's idea of a nasty joke? Is this slander? Or libel? Or is there something *more* to this crazy stunt? This is *Rock* Hamilton, reporting live on race day from the Vancouver International Holiday Marathon. We're at ten minutes before the starting gun, and we've got a showdown on our hands!"

When Rock had first announced the birds' presence, the huge crowd had gone suddenly and eerily quiet, and thousands of bodies had slowly turned *en masse* to stare. Jane heard a roaring in her ears and thought she was about to faint. Flory's cell phone rang as if from a tremendous distance, and Jane used the thready little sound to pull herself back. "Racers on the ground," Flory answered in a whisper, and then listened. "Ten-four, Mothership. Over. We've been spotted from the stands," she told the others. "Keep your eyes on the SeaKing people."

They uncovered the signs Jane and her mom had made, professionally printed in fonts designed to be readable at a hundred feet, and held them aloft above the heads of the other runners.

THIS ISN'T CRUDE, IT'S CANOLA! Jane's read.

Amy came next:

ANIMALS FOUND ALIVE: 508
ANIMALS FOUND DEAD: 182
SURVIVORS: 147

Flory brought up the rear:

> *ANIMAL RESCUE AND REHAB COSTS: $380,000*
> *COMPENSATION PAID: Ø*
> *WHY? ASK SEAKING!*

As they made their way forward, the crowd parted to let them through. They could hear whispered questions and the occasional titter, but most everyone had their eyes on the oiled birds and their ears tuned into Rock Hamilton's play-by-play. The girls never took their eyes off the SeaKing executives in the stands.

Flory hit the Send button on her cell phone the instant Alan Coyne leapt out of his seat. They watched Belinda Lee take the bleacher stairs two at a time, right behind him, followed immediately by Mason Choi and more slowly by Wayde Coyne. Flory's message was a signal to Ellen Ray that the moment had come to direct the media down to the scene at the starting line. Ellen had learned which newspapers and TV stations would be covering the race, and then narrowed down a list of reporters whom she knew would trust a tip that came from her. On Friday, she'd text-messaged the entire list, letting them know she would be in the stands on race day and that they might wish to be prepared to cover a second story before the starting gun went off. At Flory's signal just now, she sent them a second message, assuring them that the spectacle they were witnessing was in fact a genuine news story. Jane prayed, for what seemed like the millionth time, that all this would work, that the reporters would trust her mom's message, that they'd get to them on time. The SeaKing executives were almost on them.

"What is the meaning of this … this outrage?" Alan Coyne shouted, his face a mottled red and one fist raised in the air. He lunged forward as if to grab Jane by the wings and pulled up short, realizing the oil that coated them was real. The abrupt stop seemed to clear his head and remind him of where he was. He continued in quieter tones, but the color in his face and neck grew deeper. "You people can't *say* these things," he hissed. "There's nothing to 'ask SeaKing' because there's nothing to tell. That spill was an accident. An *accident*, I tell you. Take your filthy lies and get out of here now, or I'll *sue*!" Never mind sue, the distraught man looked ready to commit murder. Jane took comfort in Flory's close presence, knowing her friend had checked and rechecked the details of their plan with her uncle. They couldn't stop SeaKing from suing them, but they hadn't given the company any rope to hang them by, either.

A sinuous voice reached around in front of Alan Coyne and found its way to the girls' ears. "I've heard that chickens will run around for quite a while after you chop their heads off," the voice said.

"Easy," Alan Coyne tried to muffle the speaker. She stepped out from behind him, garbed head to toe in designer black athletic gear, blonde hair swinging. Jane suddenly caught the faint scent of something familiar, and for a second time she was afraid she might faint. She was dizzy, too hot in this suit, couldn't breathe. Couldn't breathe…

"Never heard of them running a whole marathon, though," Belinda Lee finished.

"Belinda, that's enough!" Alan barked. Perfume, that's what that smell was. Belinda's perfume. Not a man, a *woman*! A woman had been running behind her that day, had attacked her on the seawall, had left her in the water to drown. Belinda Lee. She hadn't even noticed the perfume that day—or thought she hadn't—but she recognized it now.

"We're not running the whole marathon, Blonde Joke, we're running the half!" Amy's irrepressible retort brought Jane to her senses in time to see Belinda wind herself up for some sort of martial arts move aimed directly at her. Where the hell were those TV cameras? For that matter, where was her mom?

She wasn't going down without a fight this time. On instinct, she drew herself up to her full height, shook her massive head piece and flapped her wings, shouting the first thing that came into her head: "Noooooooooooooo!" It was enough to throw the petite woman off balance. Someone caught her as she teetered backward, and pinned her arms behind her.

"Let me go," she screeched. "Let me GO!" Mason Choi had caught up with the group just in time to put a stop to Belinda's martial arts maneuvers with one of his own. Jane's gaze lighted on the logo emblazoned on the young man's sweatshirt: a three-pronged scepter capped by a crown. It was the SeaKing logo, of course, but he was the only one in the group wearing it today.

"Trident!" she gasped. Without changing his expression, he gave her the sparest wink, and then turned his attention back to the screeching Belinda.

"Shut *up*, Belinda," Alan tried one last time. "The reporters are here." He adjusted his cravat and forced a smile.

Through the barrage of questions and a lightning storm of camera flashes, above the underscore of Rock Hamilton's continuous commentary, Jane, Amy, and Flory listened as Alan Coyne reiterated the same story SeaKing had been telling since October—the accident, their heroic cleanup efforts, their continued intentions to make a donation to the Urban Wildlife Rescue Center. He regained his composure in the process, and managed to portray Jane and her friends as fringe radicals keen to disrupt a major city event just to get their names in the news. Wayde Coyne had arrived by this time, and edged up behind his uncle, nervously feeding himself doughnut holes from a half-empty box. "They have nothing but contempt for our beautiful city," Alan concluded, "for the race organizers and sponsors, or for you, the runners. No common decency, no grounds for their ridiculous charges, no ..."

"Proof," Amy finished for him. While he was talking, Amy had lowered her knapsack to the ground, unzipped the flap, and removed a large cylindrical object. Now, she hoisted it to her shoulder, and then raised it into the air.

The morning's first light bounced off the silvery metal, gleaming where the object had picked up oil from Amy's feathers, and disappearing where the metal went dark—reddish-black with rot—or was rusted completely through. It was Jim Ellis's stolen segment of corroded pipeline, recreated in exact detail in her laboratory by Amy MacGillivray. For just a moment, daylight was easily outstripped by camera flashes.

"How did they get that?" Wayde Coyne breathed, almost inaudibly, into his uncle's ear. "I took them all. I took them all!" Alan Coyne's confident, smiling face went slack with shock and understanding. He bent his head slowly forward and placed it in trembling hands.

"Got it!" one reporter crowed, waving a microphone above Wayde Coyne's head. "Keep filming!"

The television spotlight found Wayde, and Jane spied a determined group of security guards making their way quickly toward the scrum. Rock Hamilton continued to commentate, live, on air, from fabulous downtown Vancouver, and announced that he'd convinced race organizers to postpone the start of the whole event by fifteen minutes.

She glanced up at the sponsor stands one last time. Jake and his father were gone. Amy caught her eye and shrugged, and Flory shook her head. A mystery for another time, maybe. One was enough for today. They had to get themselves out of these costumes—they had a race to run.

32
FLIGHT

JANE HAD STUDIED THE MAP that came with her race package, and run the course at least twenty times in her head. So when she turned off Georgia Street and into Stanley Park, she knew she was half way to the finish line. The first six miles had taken her east from the Plaza of Nations, through the old Strathcona neighborhood and then over the railroad tracks to Coal Harbour before she emerged onto Georgia's main thoroughfare. The half-marathon leaders were far ahead of her, there was a big group of joggers and walkers behind her, and she'd watched, amazed, as the champion marathon runners, who'd started fifteen minutes after her, passed her and disappeared into the distance.

1:04. One hour and four minutes. If she managed to maintain her pace, she'd finish in 2:08, a personal best and two minutes under her goal. It seemed almost too much to ask after the morning's earlier success, but she wasn't about to say no to the gift.

She spotted the official race photographers positioned in front of the Rowing Club, and tried to grin before having to accept that her face just didn't get any wider. Laughing out loud to give the joy somewhere to go, she grabbed Flory's hand on her left and Amy's on her right and held them high as they ran by the cameras.

That's what she remembered later about the Holiday Half Marathon—smiling for two solid hours. That, and the smell of a salt-blue breeze blowing in from the Pacific Ocean, the "hellos" and "keep it ups" and jokes of other runners, the people four times her age who passed her with ease, their white hair and sexy, muscled calves surprising her and planting the seed of a new goal in her mind, the certainty at mile ten that her own tired legs could not possibly keep going, and the fact that they did. And Flory on her left and Amy on her right, running with her, step for step, all the way.

When they reached a point on the seawall about half way between the Mermaid and the Lion's Gate Bridge, Jane angled her body seaward, placed her palms together in front of her chest, and gave a slight bow. The rescues—the scoter's and her own—had rendered the place sacred. Unmarked though it was, she would never again pass it without thinking on those two events and everything that they'd led to.

Amy's breath-heavy voice inserted itself into the rhythm of their steps. "Your little ninja move there just reminded me, Jane … Did you see the look on Belinda's face when you pulled off your scoter head-piece? You could tell she was sure she'd killed you that day, whether she meant to or not. She looked like she'd seen a ghost!" Jane had told them both how she'd guessed the identity of her attacker.

"I just wish we'd gotten here in time to see it that day," Flory added. "With no witnesses, we can never prove what happened. I'm afraid recognizing some-body's perfume isn't admissible as legal evidence."

"I'll probably always wonder why Belinda attacked me," Jane said, "but I've got all the proof I need to know for sure that she did." She looked sideways at Flory. "And you guys know what happened." She glanced back over her shoulder at the Mermaid. "And so does she." Jane winked at the silent statue, trying to make her face a blank the way Trident had. But she couldn't do it. The smile just wouldn't go away.

Under the bridge and around to the west face of Stanley Park, past Siwash Rock and out of the park to English Bay, under the Burrard Street bridge and a loop at Hornby and then up to Pacific Boulevard for the final stretch to the finish line. The streets were lined with people cheering and waving and shouting encouragement to runners who were literally on their last legs. What had gotten *them* out of bed before 9:00 a.m. on a Sunday to do this? How long had they been there? Jane would remember that, too—the feeling of being held and helped along by people she'd never met and would likely never see again.

Feeling a light splash on her cheeks, she scanned the crowd, trying to see who was wielding the spritzer bottle. "It's snowing!" Flory squealed. "Look up! Look up! It's snowing!" It was. The flakes were small and sparse at first, and fell slowly, as if undecided about leaving the soft, gray sky for cold, hard ground. But they stuck. Soon the road was coated with a featherlight blanket of white, and as volunteers scurried to toss sand and salt on the race course, the flakes gathered together in clusters on the way down and began to fall thickly, and fast.

With the first few flakes, the crowd had fallen silent, and all heads tilted back to look up in wonder at the sight. In the hush, the only sound was the muffled crunch of the runners' shoes on new snow. But as the flakes grew and gathered speed, all eyes returned to the runners, and the cheering began again, louder than before. The shouts and cries grew wild as the onlookers in the approaching stands raised their voices with those lining the road to carry the racers to the finish line.

The chutes were still at least a hundred yards away when Jane spotted the bright yellow of her mom's jacket through the falling snow. "Mom!" she tried to yell, but her voice stuck in her throat. She and Flory and Amy had joined hands when the chutes had first come into view. Now, Jane gave them each a squeeze before letting go to surge ahead. A few seconds later, both girls were at her sides again, holding their own at the faster pace, and grinning. They were going to cross that finish line together no matter what.

Jane's mom was dancing and waving her arms and pointing at something on the other side of the chute. Something, or some*one* ... Was it ... no. Was it her dad? A few steps closer. It was. It was her dad! He must have closed the restaurant. Her mom stood on one side of the center chute and her dad on the other, both of them jumping up and down like little kids and screaming with the rest of the crowd. As they approached the finish, Flory veered to the chute on Jane's left and Amy to the one on her right. Jane glanced up at the clock—2:07—and then back at her mom and dad, unable to stop grinning even through tears. She entered the chute, and as she ran the last few steps to the finish line, she felt her feet leave the ground, and she flew.

33
A LITTLE MORE FAME

THE SHACK might as well have been the call-in center for a TV telethon. It was Monday after school, and Jane, Amy, and Flory had retreated to the old garden shed as soon as they were able to tear themselves away from the crowds at school. Every student at Cedar's Ridge Senior Secondary, it seemed, had watched Sunday night's news and wanted to hear the story again straight from the girls themselves. Now, both Flory's cell and the old red rotary phone Amy had wired up from the house were ringing non-stop, and Jane sat shaking her head, wide-eyed, as her friends fielded call after call.

Classmates who hadn't managed to stall them in the halls called on their cell phones from the bus as they headed home. Avis called to speak to Jane. "I was convinced the plan would work, Jane, but I must say it tickled me pink to see you pull it off right in front of my eyes. See you at the Center next week!" Ray, MacGillivray, and Morales relatives called from across town, from Scotland, from the Philippines. Flory cried as she talked to her parents and her sisters, and described in detail the role the family law firm had played in their plan. Jane stepped outside to give her some privacy, and to get away from the ringing and the chatter.

"Jane!" Amy stuck her head out the door. "Call for you! It's Farmer Mike!" He'd been away at an organic farming workshop on Cortes Island for the weekend. Jane grinned and dove back into the chaos, grabbing the receiver out of Amy's hand.

"Do they let you have a TV out there in the sticks, or did you hear all about it over short-wave radio?" Jane spoke before Mike could say hello. He laughed.

"I saw it all with my own two flabbergasted eyes," he said. "You were three hot chicks, I've gotta say!"

"Some farmer you're going to be, if you thought we were chickens!" she teased, trying to deflect the unexpected compliment from her old friend. Why on earth was she blushing?

"I grow vegetables! What do I know about chickens? Seriously, Jane, I wish I'd been there in person. You must have been something to see." His voice sober, he added, "Any idea what's going to happen to those SeaKing people? I can't imagine you're safe until that crazy kung fu lady's in a padded cell somewhere." Jane had been wondering the same thing herself, and was listening with her other ear to Flory as she conversed with her uncle on the cell. Morales & Monroy had taken on the case against SeaKing, and would have spent the day questioning the four executives. If they hadn't managed to glean enough evidence to detain them, Belinda Lee and the others would be free to go by this evening.

"Actually, Flory's on the phone with her uncle right now. I'll probably know a lot more in half an hour. Would … can I … if … should I, um, call you back?" Oh, for crying out loud, why did the idea of calling him back have her stuttering? A simple phone call. Only she realized she'd never called Mike MacGillivray in her life before. Sure, she'd spoken to him on the phone a million times, but only as a precursor to talking to Amy. She told herself to get a grip. It was just Mike.

"Yeah, actually. Please do." They made plans for Jane to call him back that evening, and she hoped no one noticed she was blushing. Stupid cheeks. Stupid phone call. Why was she looking forward to it? Stupid Mike.

Flory flipped her cell phone closed and raised wide eyes to Jane and Amy. "Can of worms. Pandora's Box. Kettle of fish. You name it, these SeaKing people fit the bill." She leveled a gaze at Jane. "Your little scoter has changed a lot of people's lives." Jane felt a shiver run down her spine. He had certainly changed hers.

"Well, tell us! *What*, already?" Amy pleaded, exasperated. "Are they in jail? Have they denied everything? Is your uncle pressing for the death penalty? *What*?"

"They're in *custody*, everybody's spilling their beans, and no, Amy, Canada abolished the death penalty in 1976. But it looks like at least one of them is going to prison for a while."

Flory told them what had come to light as each of the SeaKing executives had undergone questioning. Wayde's admission in front of the cameras on Sunday indicated that SeaKing had been negligent in using a pipeline that was in poor repair. A search of his North Vancouver property proved it—he had kept all of the corroded pieces of pipeline he'd taken from the warehouse that night back in October. Alan Coyne's company, which he'd carefully and lovingly built over twenty-five years of his life, would be fined a sum large enough to cover the costs of the cleanup of the spill as well as animal rescue and rehabilitation—well over half a million dollars—and in addition would likely be required to pay a much larger sum to the City of Vancouver, which would be held in trust for the establishment of a special new fund. "More on that in a minute," Flory said. Amy groaned.

The senior Coyne, who had been planning to retire next year, realized he would have to downsize the company significantly if it was going to survive the financial setback of the fines, or perhaps even sell it. Either way, SeaKing was unlikely to be a going concern again for a long time to come. In a shocking move, he offered through his lawyer to turn the company over to Mason Choi. "I knew my nephew's heart was never in it," he apparently said, "and after yesterday, I don't think he's fit to run a company. But I always trusted that Choi fellow. He's got a good head on his shoulders." Mason, however, politely refused Alan's offer, saying the oil business wasn't for him and that he'd already decided to quit, after which Alan announced that he would be winding down SeaKing's affairs permanently. As soon as the necessary paperwork was complete, SeaKing Shipping Pacific would no longer exist.

"Hmm … too bad," Amy mused aloud. "A worthy opponent really brings out the chutzpah in Jane!"

The strange comment surprised a laugh out of Jane. Amy could always be counted on for a unique perspective on things. "As long as I love animals," she said, "I'm sure there will always be opponents, worthy or otherwise."

Flory nodded. "Oddly enough, Wayde Coyne is an animal lover, too. You'd never know it by his actions. But then, nothing's turned out to be what it seemed on the surface." Flory told them about the history between Wayde and Alan Coyne, and that Wayde's decision to replace the corroded pipeline joints with intact ones was prompted by a very longstanding wish to repay his uncle for saving his life. When he was told of the likelihood of a prison sentence for tampering with evidence, obstruction of justice, and the cover-up of a negligent act that had resulted in serious eco-logical devastation, he wasn't upset or angry, or even afraid. He seemed, in fact, relieved. He asked to see his uncle, and explained that he'd never wanted to work in the shipping industry, that he'd done it only to please him, and that his dream since childhood was to be a poet. By switching the pipeline segments, he felt he'd finally repaid his debt to his uncle and could live his own life. Jail, he felt, would give him an opportunity to hone his craft without the need to earn money for food or clothing, and his only regret was that he couldn't take his cat, Jelly, with him.

Once he understood the financial implications of Alan's situation, Wayde offered his uncle the use of his home while he served his sentence. Alan seemed bewildered by the younger man's simplistic grasp of what had happened, and grieved that Wayde had committed a criminal act in a twisted effort to help him. Wayde never apologized, seeing his actions only from within his own limited agenda. But Alan embraced his nephew, and forgave him, before they were separated once again by officials.

"That is the weirdest thing I have ever heard," Amy said, shaking her head.

"I don't know," Jane said quietly. "Wouldn't you do anything for your family? I would."

"Not that!" Amy responded, shocked. "I wouldn't cover for them if they did something bad—no way!"

Flory looked from one to the other. "I'm with Jane. I mean, I don't know what I'd do in that situation, but believe me, lots of crimes are committed to cover up others, all in the name of love. The law is powerful, but it's nothing compared to human emotion."

"Speaking of which, what about Belinda?" Jane was almost afraid to ask, but wanted to know what would become of her attacker.

"An interesting case," Flory agreed. When officials questioned her about her knowledge of SeaKing's negligence, she exploded into heaving sobs, and it took four police officers, two boxes of tissues and a tall, extra-hot, no-foam latté to comfort her and calm her down. It seemed the expensively dressed executive with the traffic-stopping long blonde hair had only just recently left a dismal life of poverty behind her. Immigrants from China, her parents had arrived penniless in Vancouver and taken up residence in a basement suite in Chinatown. Medical professionals in their former life, her parents were not legally allowed to practise here in Canada, and were forced to start from scratch in menial jobs just to buy the bare necessities for their children. Belinda and her younger brother often went to bed hungry, and they slept with the covers tucked over their heads to keep out the rats that scuttled through the basement during the night. Instead of being grateful to her parents for their sacrifices, Belinda had clearly grown bitter about all that she felt her life was lacking, and resolved to leave her family's struggle and squalor behind as soon as the right opportunity came along.

Flory's uncle peppered the woman with questions about Jane's attack, trying to cause her to slip up and admit something, but she broke down in tears again, and one of the attending officers positioned himself protectively in front of her and told the lawyer to back off. In the end, she convinced the officers—if not Flory's uncle—that she'd kept suspicions about a corroded pipeline to herself in part to protect her beloved employer and in part to protect her job. She had gotten herself out of poverty by her own ingenuity, she said, and she was damned if she was going back. Flory's uncle had to admit she made a compelling, if rather dramatic, case for herself, and suspected she'd eventually get off with a small fine and a slap on the wrist. She definitely knew how to play the system.

"Yeah, well, just as long as she doesn't try anything with Jane again," Amy scowled.

"What about Trident?" Jane broke in. She didn't want to think about Belinda Lee any more. In this case, realizing the truth about her attack hadn't brought her any closer to justice, and she was going to have to figure out how to live with that.

Flory chuckled. "My uncle said he was the only one of the four who didn't behave like an actor from a TV crime show!" Calmly and quietly, without looking his interrogators in the eye, Mason had answered every question in a simple, straightforward way, and offered his own information whenever there were gaps in the story. He explained that they had all known about the corroded pipeline from the first day after the spill. Alan, his boss, never asked any of them to cover up that fact, but did ask them to stick to the story of an accidental puncture at least until they had the results of the official inspection. To everyone's surprise, the inspector found the pipeline to be in good working condition, with the exception of one punctured joint, concluded the damage had been caused by external forces, and exonerated SeaKing of any responsibility for the spill. Alan was more than happy to accept the inspector's report at face value, but Mason suspected a cover-up. Wayde had made it clear that first day that the dock workers had found the pipeline in terrible condition. The problem was, Mason didn't know where to turn with his suspicions. "I was right when I said someone at SeaKing was on your side, you see," Flory said. "His parents and grandparents had raised him to fear the authorities. It never occurred to him to go the police. So he did the next best thing—he went to Jane." She smiled at Jane. "My uncle will want to talk to you, to corroborate the Trident story," she explained. "And so will the police. But it looks like his attempts to bring the truth to light will make things easier for him."

"I hope so," Jane said. "He helped save my life."

"What a mess!" Amy exclaimed. "Like it wasn't bad enough to spill fifty tonnes of oil into Burrard Inlet in the first place, they had to go and make it worse—for the dock workers, for the animals, even for themselves!"

Flory nodded again. "If you can believe it, though, some good might just come out of it all. For one thing, Jim Ellis's severance payments will continue for as long as it takes him to find a new job. Which won't be long—he's already had offers from two progressive companies that want honest guys like him running their operations. And..." She paused dramatically, and waited until Amy rolled her eyes. "Your plan worked, Jane... "

"You mean *our* plan," Jane interrupted. "I didn't do any of this by myself. I would have been under the bedcovers with Sweet Pea and Minnie for three months straight if it hadn't been for you guys and Avis and my mom and Trident and … everybody!"

"Sure, Jane, whatever you say." Flory waved her protest away. "The bottom line is, it worked. The UWRC is going to recover their costs for all the animals they treated, which means Daniel gets his job back, and—it gets better—my family's firm is spearheading the creation of a lobby group to press for the creation of a city-wide oil spill emergency response plan!"

Jane gasped. "Are you serious?"

"Oh, yes. They want oil companies—of all kinds—to contribute every year to a protected account so that there's a pre-planned, funded response to spills. No more total chaos and cash shortages like what happened this time!"

"What about restaurants with oil dumps out back? What about boaters like…" She'd started to say the Harbinsales, but stopped herself. "Like at Cultus?"

Flory shook her head slightly. "One step at a time, my friend. This is huge."

"Oh, I know!" Jane was actually overwhelmed by the incredible implications of the idea. "Do you think the UWRC could be a part of it?"

"They already are!" Flory crowed. "My uncle contacted Evie this morning, and the Center will work with the lobby group and government and with members of the city councils throughout the Lower Mainland to help create an emergency response plan that puts animals and their habitats first."

Jane could hardly take it all in. A plan like Flory was talking about wouldn't stop spills from happening, but it would make companies think about the effects of their actions beyond how much money they lost in spilled oil. And it would give more animals a fighting chance at survival after a spill.

"So…? What do you think?" Jane realized Flory was waiting for a response from her.

"It's … it's …"

The red phone rang. The three of them groaned. Amy answered it, and then held the receiver out to Jane. "It's for you."

"*Not here!*" Jane mouthed. "*Take a message!*"

"It's Evie again," Amy said. "Your mom must have told her where you were." Jane reached for the phone.

"Jane, hi, it's Evie. Listen, we have a scaup here that's ready for release, and I was wondering whether you'd be available to drive down to Stanley Park this afternoon." Jane glanced at her watch. 3:30. Lots of time to get downtown before dark. And yet suddenly, she felt utterly exhausted. All she wanted to do was crash on the couch at home with the cats and a mug of hot cocoa. She closed her eyes and mustered the strength to say yes—there probably wasn't anything Evie could ask that she'd refuse. Evie must have sensed her hesitation, though, because she spoke again before Jane had managed to find her voice.

"He was actually ready to go yesterday, but I waited because I thought you might want to be the one to do it."

"Evie, did you say it was a scaup?" Jane asked. She thought back to last Thursday's shift and couldn't remember seeing any scaups on the board or in the Care Center. Oh, wait … except one. The one that had been there since October, since the day she'd arrived with her scoter. The one that had rallied and almost died of infection and then slowly recovered again.

"Yeah," Evie chuckled softly. "It's Scotty."

34
RELEASE

JANE FLICKED THE RADIO ON and listened to the car fill with voices—war, oil prices, the Olympic village, fur fashions, drought. She switched it off. She'd had all the news she needed today. She heard a knocking sound and glanced back to see the cardboard kennel shifting and hopping as the scaup rebelled against the sudden confinement. At the next red light, she reached back and replaced the towel over the kennel, and the bird grew calm. "Easy, Scotty. You're almost home," she said quietly.

Her mind drifted back over everything Flory had told them this afternoon. So many lives had changed—her own, her family's and friends', the SeaKing executives', people she didn't even know. Some for worse, much worse. Some—like Jim Ellis's, like her own—for the better. And this fund Flory had proposed, for an emergency response plan. It meant changes for animals. Definitely for the better. Butterfly effect, Mike had called it. Some butterfly.

She felt more like a pterodactyl.

She wondered suddenly if she had kept silent these past four years, not because the things she said made no difference, but because of some inkling that they might make a very big difference indeed. Had some part of her known all along, even while she was hiding in her room with Sweet Pea and Minnie, even while she was running alone through the woods, that one day she would speak, and that things would change? That her life would change?

When she tried to understand *what* had changed, she couldn't name it. She hadn't taken a step closer to becoming a lawyer, like Flory, or a science teacher, like Amy. She didn't think it would make sense to too many people if she tried to explain that she'd taken one step closer to becoming Jane Ray.

A rattling from the back seat brought her back to West Georgia Street in rush hour and the entrance to Stanley Park. She passed the Rowing Club on her right, and beyond it, the little floating gas stations she'd always loved, but looked at differently now. Turning left into the Brockton Oval parking lot, she cut across to the north wall and parked the car.

A brisk winter wind that smelled of pine forests and snow blew down from the North Shore mountains and whipped her hair. She reached into the back seat and retrieved Scotty's kennel, careful to keep it covered with the towel, and headed down the seawall toward Lumberman's Arch.

A short distance past the Mermaid, she spotted a group of scaups and scoters and buffleheads swimming idly and preening a short distance from shore. Perfect. The tide was still coming in, and there was a sandy stretch between the wall and the waves where she could put Scotty down to acclimate. She found a set of stone steps leading down to the sand and walked to the edge of the water. Setting the kennel down on the sand, she stepped back to the wall and waited, giving Scotty time to get used to sights and sounds and smells he hadn't encountered for over three months.

After a few minutes, she returned to the kennel and, taking a deep breath, gently tilted the box toward the water's edge, unhooked the flaps, and opened them wide. Scotty found a wave, and then his wings, and was in the air.

Up and out over the water he flew, letting the wind do the work for him, circling above the Mermaid and then low over the ducks as if testing his welcome. He returned for a languorous loop above Jane's head before swooping down to join the little mixed flock, webbed feet pressed forward and wings held back to slow his descent and brace his landing between two other scaups.

Jane strained to keep her focus on him, keep him separate from the others, but he wouldn't cooperate. He was swimming circles and figure eights with the other scaups and trading places with them behind small swells in the sea.

Release him, she thought. *You're supposed to release him.*

She closed her eyes for a moment, and when she opened them again she saw a flock of wild seabirds bobbing and turning in the windswept waves. One of them — she no longer knew which — had almost died in an oil spill, had been held captive in a little hospital in the woods for over three months where she and a hundred others had joined him in his fight to survive.

And now he was free.

Flory's Files

I really wanted to call this section "Top Secret," but Jane said, "What's the point of doing all that research if you're not going to share it with everybody?" She has a point. So here are a few of the files I've opened since the oil spill. Take notes—you might decide to open a file of your own!

File #0509001
Surf Scoter

I found the surf scoter description that so amused Jane and Amy in a book called *Birds of Coastal British Columbia* by Nancy Baron and John Acorn. Lone Pine Publishing (Vancouver), 1997, pp. 74–75. This is just one of many great reference books on identifying and understanding birds and wildlife. Check out your library for more—you may even find a few dedicated to the animals of your own region!

File #0509002
How to Find a Wildlife Rehabilitation Center Near You

The best place to start is with your provincial or national rehabilitation network's website. Once you're there, find the rehabilitation center closest to your community. Then make sure to keep the address and phone number in a safe, prominent place—maybe on your fridge or with the emergency numbers in your phone book—so you can find it easily when you need it.

File #0509002 (cont.)

Here are a few URLs to get you started:

International Wildlife
Rehabilitation Council
http://www.iwrc-online.org
The mission of the IWRC is conserving and protecting wildlife and habitat through wildlife rehabilitation.

National Wildlife
Rehabilitators Association
http://www.nwrawildlife.org/home.asp
The NWRA is dedicated to improving and promoting the profession of wildlife rehabilitation and its contributions to preserving natural ecosystems.

Wildlife Rehabilitators Network
of British Columbia
http://www.wrn.bc.ca
The mission of the WRNBC is to advocate for wildlife through appropriate action, legislation, and education.

Wildlife Rescue Association
of British Columbia
http://www.wildliferescue.ca
The Wildlife Rescue Association of BC provides leadership in the care and rehabilitation of injured, orphaned, and pollution-damaged wildlife, primarily in the Lower Mainland of British Columbia, Canada. It is also committed to raising public awareness of, and respect for, wildlife and the issues affecting them in the urban environment.

Oil Spill

Now that you know something about what can happen to wild animals caught in an oil spill, you might also be interested to know there are things you can do to help! Check out these websites for more information on oil spill response, and contact your local wildlife rehabilitation center to find out how you can get involved.

International Bird Rescue and
Research Center (California)
http://www.ibrrc.org
The mission of the IBRRC is to mitigate human impact on aquatic birds and other wildlife. They accomplish their goals through rehabilitation, emergency response, education, research, planning, and training.

Oiled Wildlife Society of
British Columbia
http://www.vcn.bc.ca/owsbc/
The mission of the OWSBC is to create a high level of emergency preparedness and awareness of oiled wildlife caused by oil spills.

Burrard Clean Operations
http://www.burrardclean.com
Burrard Clean Operations is a privately run company that is hired by its clients to provide prevention and preparedness training as well as marine spill response.

What to Do If You Find Injured, Orphaned, or Oiled Wildlife

The chances for survival of a sick or injured wild bird or mammal can be greatly increased by the response of the person who finds it—that could be you!

If you find a sick, injured, or oiled bird, wrap it gently in a light towel or cloth, put it in a covered, ventilated cardboard box (or cage) and keep their environment warm, dark, and quiet. Handle the animal as little as possible, if at all. Stress is the biggest danger to wildlife in captivity. Contrary to our nurturing instincts, being handled, petted, and talked to are all unnatural and terrifying for them, and can even be fatal.

The faster you can get the animal to a wildlife rehabilitation facility, the better its chances for survival. Infections spread rapidly, fractures can start to heal in the wrong position, and even a day without food may be too much for the small and weak. Help conserve their energy by keeping them warm. Get them to help as soon as possible.

Most importantly, do *not* try to treat the animal yourself. Professional rehabilitators have access to appropriate diets, caging, and medical care.

Wild mammals and even birds can be dangerous, especially when cornered and injured. Call your local rehabilitation center to discuss the situation and find out how to proceed safely. A professional rehabilitator can instruct you on proper methods of capture, transport, and emergency care. In some cases, such as with fledgling birds, your intervention may not be necessary. A rehabilitator may even be able to help you resolve the problem over the phone!

How to Make Your Own
Animal Rescue Kit

You will need the following:

- a ventilated box that can be securely closed, or a cage or kennel with a solid floor
- some old towels and blankets
- an electric heating pad
- work gloves (to keep you safe!)

Line the box or cage with a soft towel, have a second towel on hand for wrapping the animal, and keep another large towel aside for creating a drape once the animal is inside the container. When you find a sick or injured animal, wear your gloves and wrap the animal gently in a light-colored towel, making sure to cover its head. Place it in the lined container, releasing it from the towel as you do so. Cover the box with the drape, and call your local wildlife rehabilitator for further instructions. If it is after hours, keep the animal warm by placing the covered box on the heating pad on "low." Do not touch or talk to the animal, or give it anything to eat or drink. Keep it in a room separate from house pets. The next morning, take the animal directly to your wildlife rehabilitator.

ACKNOWLEDGEMENTS

To all the staff and volunteers of the Wildlife Rescue Association of BC: Mike Armstrong, Janice Dickie, Nikki Fried, Devin Manky, Pam Morris, Gail Telfer, Roy Teo, Anya Smith, and Jackie Ward for the training and learning opportunities, your remarkable patience, support, and encouragement of all the volunteers, and for your own dedication to the animals. To Zoë Renaud for the comprehensive training manual, to which I referred many times during the writing of *Flight or Fight*, and for that first, memorable training session. To Mary Bruneau, Gaynor Jordan, Gloria Norton, Nicole Ponte, Crystal Simmons, and Josée Tremblay for coffee and everything that goes with it, and to Irving Lau and Paul Steeves. And to the animals, whose spirit, resilience, and ability to heal against the odds are the ultimate inspiration.

To Jackie, Janice, FOCUS Wildlife, the Oiled Wildlife Society and Burrard Clean for making oiled animal rescue and rehabilitation training available to 70 volunteers in 2004.

To Jackie Ward, Liz Thunstrom, and Monica Cirera for reading and correcting early drafts of the manuscript. Any errors that remain are most certainly mine.

To all of my wild and wonderful friends, especially: Mark Allder, who always knows when to call; Teenie Turner Armstrong, who was there when it happened; Bonzo the Great, who saved my life; Susan Baerg, for all the years and for sharing the rough stuff; Jan Bell-Irving, for always speaking straight from her soul; Gomez Caetano, for reminding me we're all healers; Lauren Chan and Lou Isidoro, for comfort food and comforting conversation at the Garden; Alex Crabtree, for the perfectly timed rose; Cam and Danae Dagg, for getting me out on the town; Chris Dahl, for four years of earthly sustenance; Tad Dick, avatar extraordinaire; Dr. G, for reminding me that I can choose to sit on either side of the desk; Russ Hamilton, for Rock, and for showing me how to draw a line; Elena Kyriacou, for being the first to know, and to celebrate; Lisa Manfield, for joining me in the *Conversations*; Allison Markin, for demonstrating what it means to hang in there; Pat at Tyax for showing me that you never know how far your voice will carry; Jill Prince, for being the first champion of my still small voice, and for the laptop, without which this book *still* would not be written; Gordon Roberts and Marni Johnson, for taking care of me in all ways; Valerie Rose, mentor, friend, and Dancing Queen; Patricia Seto, for remembering *everything*; Amy Stephen, for always demonstrating what it means to be true to oneself; Paul Tessier, for the best gift I ever received; Lori Thiessen, for the Molly M'Aidez Society and home-cooked wisdom; Tina, for helping me never forget; and Shandi Warkentin, for deepening the friendship. Special thanks to Kimberley Alcock, who has been my writing partner for many years, for her creativity, inspiration, and wholehearted celebration of every little success along the way.

To my teachers, including authors who inspired me in the writing of this first book: Georgina Eden, Candace Frank, Tannis Gough, and Trisha Horne; Enid Blyton, Jean Estoril, Carolyn Keene (in all her incarnations), Barbara Kingsolver, cartoonist Patrick McDonnell, and Tamora Pierce.

To David Fraser and Dan Weary of UBC's Animal Welfare program, for helping to make animals' security, comfort, and happiness a priority academically, socially, and politically.

To Robert McCullough, for everything and particularly for this opportunity of a lifetime, to Roberta Batchelor, Ben D'Andrea, Sonnet Force, AnnMarie MacKinnon, Robin Rivers, Alicia Schlag, Five Seventeen, Helen Stortini, Jacqui Thomas, Aydin Virani, Ian Whitelaw, and everyone at Whitecap for all their support.

To my family—especially Avis Moore, Apha Ray, and my Nana for their inspiration and guidance; to

Frances and Sadie for their constant companionship and unconditional love; to my sister Boo, who picked up her pen when I'd dropped mine, heard me asking "what about the animals?" and inspired me to write and create again; and to my parents, Don and Maryanne Haynes, upon whose return after a long absence, I flew.

And lastly, to all those who protect the small, for believing in the vision of a world that sees and values them, and for working to make it real.

Thank you.

ABOUT THE AUTHOR

Diane Haynes began volunteering with the Wildlife Rescue Association of BC after witnessing a canola oil spill in Vancouver's Burrard Inlet. First published at the age of eight, she worked as an ice cream scooper, shoe salesperson, receptionist, marketing director, and technical editor before realizing she'd had it all figured out in grade three. As a freelance feature writer, she's published stories about fashion, whales, art, TV production, an Olympic athlete, storms, mental illness, eligible bachelors, and dangerous jobs. Diane lives in Burnaby with two gray tabby cats named Sadie and Frances, and very close to a third, named Mouse. *Flight or Fight* is her first young adult novel.